THE REX ST

REX STOUT

25719-6 ★ IN U.S. $4.99 (IN CANADA $5.99) ★ A BANTAM CRIME LINE BOOK

A NERO WOLFE MYSTERY

BLACK ORCHIDS

INTRODUCTION BY LAWRENCE BLOCK

Rex Stout

REX STOUT, the creator of Nero Wolfe, was born in Noblesville, Indiana, in 1886, the sixth of nine children of John and Lucetta Todhunter Stout, both Quakers. Shortly after his birth, the family moved to Wakarusa, Kansas. He was educated in a country school, but by the age of nine he was recognized throughout the state as a prodigy in arithmetic. Mr. Stout briefly attended the University of Kansas, but left to enlist in the Navy, and spent the next two years as a warrant officer on board President Theodore Roosevelt's yacht. When he left the Navy in 1908, Rex Stout began to write free-lance articles and worked as a sightseeing guide and as an itinerant bookkeeper. Later he devised and implemented a school banking system which was installed in four hundred cities and towns throughout the country. In 1927 Mr. Stout retired from the world of finance and, with the proceeds of his banking scheme, left for Paris to write serious fiction. He wrote three novels that received favorable reviews before turning to detective fiction. His first Nero Wolfe novel, *Fer-de-Lance*, appeared in 1934. It was followed by many others, among them *Too Many Cooks*, *The Silent Speaker*, *If Death Ever Slept*, *The Doorbell Rang* and *Please Pass the Guilt*, which established Nero Wolfe as a leading character on a par with Erle Stanley Gardner's famous protagonist, Perry Mason. During World War II, Rex Stout waged a personal campaign against Nazism as chairman of the War Writers' Board, master of ceremonies of the radio program "Speaking of Liberty," and member of several national committees. After the war he turned his attention to mobilizing public opinion against the wartime use of thermonuclear devices, was an active leader in the Authors' Guild, and resumed writing his Nero Wolfe novels. Rex Stout died in 1975 at the age of eighty-eight. A month before his death, he published his seventy-second Nero Wolfe mystery, *A Family Affair*. Ten years later, a seventy-third Nero Wolfe mystery was discovered and published in *Death Times Three*.

The Rex Stout Library

Fer-de-Lance
The League of Frightened Men
The Rubber Band
The Red Box
Too Many Cooks
Some Buried Caesar
Over My Dead Body
Where There's a Will
Black Orchids
Not Quite Dead Enough
The Silent Speaker
Too Many Women
And Be a Villain
The Second Confession
Trouble in Triplicate
In the Best Families
Three Doors to Death
Murder by the Book
Curtains for Three
Prisoner's Base
Triple Jeopardy
The Golden Spiders
The Black Mountain
Three Men Out
Before Midnight
Might As Well Be Dead
Three Witnesses
If Death Ever Slept
Three for the Chair
Champagne for One
And Four to Go
Plot It Yourself
Too Many Clients
Three at Wolfe's Door
The Final Deduction
Gambit
Homicide Trinity
The Mother Hunt
A Right to Die
Trio for Blunt Instruments
The Doorbell Rang
Death of a Doxy
The Father Hunt
Death of a Dude
Please Pass the Guilt
A Family Affair
Death Times Three
The Hand in the Glove
Double for Death
Bad for Business
The Broken Vase
The Sound of Murder
Red Threads
The Mountain Cat Murders

REX STOUT

Black Orchids

Introduction
by Lawrence Block

BANTAM BOOKS
NEW YORK • TORONTO • LONDON • SYDNEY • AUCKLAND

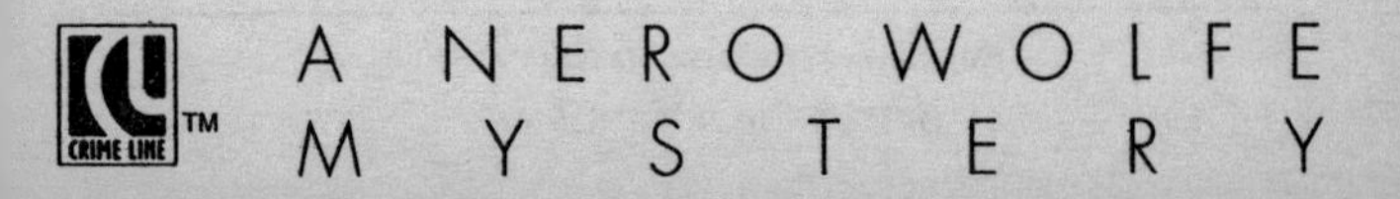

Published by The Reader's Digest Association, Inc., 1995,
by permission of Bantam Books, a division of
Bantam Doubleday Dell Publishing Group, Inc.

BLACK ORCHIDS
A Bantam Crime Line Book / published by arrangement with
the estate of the author

PUBLISHING HISTORY

Farrar & Rinehart edition published 1942
Jove / HBJ edition published January 1979
Bantam edition / May 1982
Bantam reissue / June 1992

ISBN 0-553-25719-6

Published simultaneously in the United States and Canada

Bantam Books are published by Bantam Books, a division of Bantam Doubleday Dell Publishing Group, Inc. Its trademark, consisting of the words "Bantam Books" and the portrayal of a rooster, is Registered in U.S. Patent and Trademark Office and in other countries. Marca Registrada. Bantam Books, 1540 Broadway, New York, New York 10036.

PRINTED IN THE UNITED STATES OF AMERICA

OPM 10 9 8 7 6 5 4

Introduction

In the early seventies I found myself at an impasse with a character named Chip Harrison. I had written two books about him. In the first he had lost his innocence, and in the second he was sort of looking around trying to figure out what had become of it. I wanted to write more about him, having found his voice an engaging one, but I didn't see how I could put the poor dope through another loss of innocence.

Inspiration struck, as it now and then does. Instead of having him contend with problems of his own, I'd let him stick his nose into those of other people. I'd put him to work for a private detective. Then, like all private eyes, he could stay the same age forever, and I could write about him till the cows came home.

His new employer, Leo Haig, had eked out a living in the Bronx as a small-time breeder of tropical fishes until a legacy allowed him to pursue a lifelong dream. He would become a private detective like his idol, Nero Wolfe.

Haig, a devout mystery fan, is secure in the knowledge that Nero Wolfe actually exists, not in fiction but in fact, and that the many books about him are indeed the subtly fictionalized reports of actual cases, written by Archie Goodwin himself and published under the painfully transparent pen name of "Rex Stout." (Look at the name itself, Haig says. Rex is Latin for king, Stout means fat, so what could the pseudonym be but a reference to the regal corpulence of the great detective?)

Of course, Haig would tell you, Goodwin has fictionalized things. He provides a number of addresses for the legendary brownstone, any of which would fall somewhere in the Hudson River. He calls the newspaper the *Gazette* and has Archie go dancing at the Flamingo or chasing around to the Hotel Churchill.

No doubt a man with a Wolfean concern for privacy would insist on such changes, he figures. The house is not on West Thirty-fifth Street at all, and very likely in another neighborhood altogether. Surely Wolfe's name is not Wolfe, nor Goodwin's Goodwin. But it is at least as certain that the two men exist, and Leo Haig lives in hope that, if he employs Nero Wolfe's method and principles in his chosen occupation as private detective, someday he will get his reward. Someday the telephone will ring, and someday he will be summoned to that famous house. (Perhaps in the East Eighties? Haig rather thinks it might be in the East Eighties.) There he will dine on something exquisite—shad roe, perhaps, if it's in season. And there, over postprandial coffee, Wolfe will provide the ultimate accolade.

"Satisfactory," he will say, inclining his head an eighth of an inch. "Satisfactory."

Leo Haig's character came easy to me, perhaps because it has always been effortless for me to share his idée fixe. Of course Nero Wolfe exists. Who could imagine a world without him?

I know several men and women who are forever rereading the Nero Wolfe canon. They read other things as well, of course, but every month or so they'll have another go at one of Rex Stout's books. Since there are forty, it may take four or five years at this pace to get through the cycle, at which time they can start in again at the beginning.

They do this not for the plots, which are serviceable, nor for the suspense, which is a good deal short of hair-trigger even on first reading. Nor, I shouldn't think, are they hoping for fresh insight into the human condition. No, those of us who reread Rex Stout do so for the pure joy of spending a few hours in the most congenial household in American letters, and in the always engaging company of Nero Wolfe and Archie Goodwin.

The relationship of these two men, Wolfe and Goodwin, genius and man of action, is endlessly fascinating. One quickly comes to delight in Wolfe's eccentricities—the orchids, the agoraphobia, the food and drink, the vast yellow pajamas, the refusal to countenance the use of "contact" as a verb. Ultimately, though, it is less these idiosyncracies than the pair's nuances of character that keep us transfixed. We know these two, and it is a joy to see them simply being themselves.

Rex Stout knew them, too, with such clarity that he was able to write the books almost effortlessly, in a matter of weeks. His first drafts went to the printer with no need to change so much as a comma. They seem as flawless today, and utterly timeless. For all that the world has changed, for all that New York City has changed, for all that the English language itself has changed, the books don't feel dated in the least. They are so wonderfully real within themselves that they allow us to forget what time it is outside.

It always seemed to me that the very first books were a little labored, with Wolfe tending to declaim pompously at the slightest provocation. So it often is with series; it takes a while to find out what you've got hold of. It didn't take very long at all for Stout to get a firm grasp, and he never let go. *Black Orchids* is vintage Wolfe, and long a particular favorite of mine. I especially like Wolfe's greedy obstinacy in the matter of his fee, and the part where—

Enough. Nero Wolfe needs no introduction, and has been encumbered with too much of one already. Read. Enjoy. And set the book aside when you're done. In a couple of years you'll want to read it again.

—**Lawrence Block**

Contents

Black Orchids

I don't know how many guesses there have been in the past year, around bars and dinner tables, as to how Nero Wolfe got hold of the black orchids. I have seen three different ones in print—one in a Sunday newspaper magazine section last summer, one in a syndicated New York gossip column a couple of months ago, and one in a press association dispatch, at the time that a bunch of the orchids unexpectedly appeared at a certain funeral service at the Belford Memorial Chapel.

So here in this book are two separate Nero Wolfe cases, two different sets of people. The first is the low-down on how Wolfe got the orchids. The second tells how he solved another murder, but it leaves a mystery, and that's what's biting me. If anyone who knows Wolfe better than I do—but wait till you read it.

Archie Goodwin

BLACK ORCHIDS

Chapter 1

Monday at the Flower Show, Tuesday at the Flower Show, Wednesday at the Flower Show. Me, Archie Goodwin. How's that?

I do not deny that flowers are pretty, but a million flowers are not a million times prettier than one flower. Oysters are good to eat, but who wants to eat a carload?

I didn't particularly resent it when Nero Wolfe sent me up there Monday afternoon and, anyway, I had been expecting it. After all the ballyhoo in the special Flower Show sections of the Sunday papers, it was a cinch that some member of our household would have to go take a look at those orchids, and as Fritz Brenner couldn't be spared from the kitchen that long, and Theodore Horstmann was too busy in the plant rooms on the roof, and Wolfe himself could have got a job in a physics laboratory as an Immovable Object if the detective business ever played out, it looked as if I would be elected. I was.

When Wolfe came down from the plant rooms at six P.M. Monday and entered the office, I reported:

"I saw them. It was impossible to snitch a sample."

He grunted, lowering himself into his chair. "I didn't ask you to."

"Who said you did, but you expected me to. There are

three of them in a glass case and the guard has his feet glued."

"What color are they?"

"They're not black."

"Black flowers are never black. What color are they?"

"Well." I considered. "Say you take a piece of coal. Not anthracite. Cannel coal."

"That's black."

"Wait a minute. Spread on it a thin coating of open kettle molasses. That's it."

"Pfui. You haven't the faintest notion what it would look like. Neither have I."

"I'll go buy a piece of coal and we'll try it."

"No. Is the labellum uniform?"

I nodded. "Molasses on coal. The labellum is large, not as large as aurea, about like truffautiana. Cepals lanceolate. Throat tinged with orange—"

"Any sign of wilting?"

"No."

"Go back tomorrow and look for wilting on the edges of the petals. You know it, the typical wilting after pollination. I want to know if they've been pollinated."

So I went up there again Tuesday after lunch. That evening at six I added a few details to my description and reported no sign of wilting.

I sat at my desk, in front of his against the wall, and aimed a chilly stare at him.

"Will you kindly tell me," I requested, "why the females you see at a flower show are the kind of females who go to a flower show? Ninety per cent of them? Especially their legs? Does it have to be like that? Is it because, never having any flowers sent to them, they have to go there in order to see any? Or is it because—"

"Shut up. I don't know. Go back tomorrow and look for wilting."

I might have known, with his mood getting blacker every hour, all on account of three measly orchid plants, that he was working up to a climax. But I went again Wednesday, and didn't get home until nearly seven o'clock. When I entered the office he was there at his desk with two empty beer bottles on the tray and pouring a third one into the glass.

"Did you get lost?" he inquired politely.

I didn't resent that because I knew he half meant it. He has got to the point where he can't quite understand how a man can drive from 35th Street and Tenth Avenue to 44th and Lexington and back again with nobody to lead the way. I reported no wilting, and sat at my desk and ran through the stuff he had put there, and then swiveled to face him and said:

"I'm thinking of getting married."

His half-open lids didn't move, but his eyes did, and I saw them.

"We might as well be frank," I said. "I've been living in this house with you for over ten years, writing your letters, protecting you from bodily harm, keeping you awake, and wearing out your tires and my shoes. Sooner or later one of my threats to get married will turn out not to be a gag. How are you going to know? How do you know this isn't it?"

He made a noise of derision and picked up his glass.

"Okay," I said. "But you're enough of a psychologist to know what it means when a man is irresistibly impelled to talk about a girl to someone. Preferably, of course, to someone who is sympathetic. You can imagine what it means when I want to talk about her to *you*. What is uppermost in my mind is that this afternoon I saw her washing her feet."

He put the glass down. "So you went to a movie. In the afternoon. Did it occur—"

"No, sir, not a movie. Flesh and bone and skin. Have you ever been to a flower show?"

Wolfe closed his eyes and sighed.

"Anyway," I went on, "you've seen pictures of the exhibits, so you know that the millionaires and big firms do things up brown. Like Japanese gardens and rock gardens and roses in Picardy. This year Rucker and Dill, the seed and nursery company, have stolen the show. They've got a woodland glade. Bushes and dead leaves and green stuff and a lot of little flowers and junk, and some trees with white flowers, and a little brook with a pool and rocks; and it's inhabited. There's a man and a girl having a picnic. They're there all day from eleven to six thirty and from eight to ten in the evening. They pick flowers. They eat a picnic lunch. They sit on the grass and read. They play mumblety-peg. At four o'clock the man lies down and covers his face with a newspaper and takes a nap, and the girl takes off her shoes and stockings and dabbles her feet in the pool. That's when they crowd the ropes. Her face and figure are plenty good enough, but her legs are absolutely artistic. Naturally she has to be careful not to get her skirt wet, and the stream comes tumbling from the rocks into the pool. Speaking as a painter—"

Wolfe snorted. "Pah! You couldn't paint a—"

"I didn't say painting as a painter, I said speaking as a painter. I know what I like. The arrangement of lines into harmonious composition. It gets me. I like to study—"

"She is too long from the knees down."

I looked at him in amazement.

He wiggled a finger at a newspaper on the desk. "There's a picture of her in the *Post*. Her name is Anne Tracy. She's a stenographer in Rucker and Dill's office. Her favorite dish is blueberry pie with ice cream."

"She is not a stenographer!" I was on my feet. "She's a secretary! W. G. Dill's!" I found the page in the *Post*. "A damn important job. I admit they look a little long here, but it's a bad picture. Wrong angle. There was a better one in the *Times* yesterday, and an article—"

"I saw it. I read it."

"Then you ought to have an inkling of how I feel." I sat down again. "Men are funny," I said philosophically. "That girl with that face and figure and legs has been going along living with her pop and mom and taking dictation from W. G. Dill, who looks like a frog in spite of being the president of the Atlantic Horticultural Society—he was around there today—and who knew about her or paid any attention to her? But put her in a public spot and have her take off her shoes and stockings and wiggle her toes in a man-made pool on the third floor of Grand Central Palace, and what happens? Billy Rose goes to look at her. Movie scouts have to be chased off the grass of the woodland glade. Photographers engage in combat. Lewis Hewitt takes her out to dinner—"

"Hewitt?" Wolfe opened his eyes and scowled at me. "Lewis Hewitt?"

I knew that the sound of that name would churn his beer for him. Lewis Hewitt was the millionaire in whose greenhouse, on his Long Island estate, the black orchids had been produced—thereby creating in Wolfe an agony of envy that surpassed any of his previous childish performances.

"Yep," I said cheerfully. "Lew himself, in his two hundred dollar topcoat and Homburg and gloves made of the belly-skin of a baby gazelle fed on milk and honey, and a walking stick that makes your best Malacca look like a piece of an old fishing pole. I saw her go out with him less than an hour ago, just before I left. And pinned to her left shoulder was a black orchid! He must have cut it for her himself. She becomes the first female in captivity to wear a black orchid. And only last week she was typing with her lovely fingers, 'Yours of the ninth received and contents noted.'"

I grinned at him. "But Lew will have to get out the spray for the insects. Men are flocking in there who don't know a stamen from a stigma. The guy having the picnic with her inside the ropes smirks fatuously. His name is Harry Gould and he is one of Dill's gardeners. A gray-haired geezer that needs a shave gazes at her as if he was about to say his prayers—I've seen him twice. A wholesome young fellow with a serious chin wanders by and pretends he's not looking at her. His name is Fred Updegraff. Updegraff Nurseries, Erie, Pennsylvania. They've got an exhibit not far off. And there's a lot more, but chiefly there's me. Your friend Lew is going to have me to contend with. She smiled at me today without meaning to, and I blushed from head to foot. My intentions are honorable but they are not vague. Look at that picture of her and then take a slant at this." I lifted a heel to the corner of the desk and pulled my trouser leg up to the knee. "In your mind's eye strip off the shoe and sock and garter and apply your knowledge of cross-pollination. What would be the result—"

"Pfui," Wolfe said. "Don't scar the desk. You will return there tomorrow and look for edge-wilt, and you will be here at six o'clock."

But it didn't work out that way. At lunch the next day his envy and curiosity finally foamed up to the climax. He put down his coffee cup, assumed the expression of a man prepared to brave all hardship or hazard for the sake of a Cause, and told me:

"Please bring the sedan around. I'm going up there and look at those confounded freaks myself."

Chapter 2

So Thursday was my fourth day at the Flower Show in a row. It was the biggest mob of the week, and getting Nero Wolfe through and up to the fourth floor where the orchids were was like a destroyer making a way through a mine field for a battleship. We were halted a couple of times by acquaintances who wanted to exchange greetings, and as we passed the Rucker and Dill woodland glade on the third floor Wolfe stopped to look it over. There was a line of spectators three deep all the way around the ropes. Harry and Anne were playing mumblety-peg. When a flash bulb made a flare she didn't flicker an eyelash.

"Look at her teeth when she smiles," I said. "Look at her hair like fine-spun open kettle molasses. She was more self-conscious the first day or two. A year of this would spoil her. Look at the leaves on the peony bushes, turning yellow, pining away because she'll be with them only one more day—"

"They are not peonies. They are azaleas and laurel, and they have a disease."

"Call it a disease if you want to. They're pining—"

He had started off, and I nearly knocked three women down getting around in front of him for interference.

At the orchid benches up on the fourth floor he disregarded everything else—though there was, for one thing, the finest display of B. thorntoni I had ever seen—and planted himself in front of the glass case. A card in the corner said, "Unnamed hybrid by Mr. Lewis Hewitt. The only three plants in existence." They certainly were something different, and I had been through all the big establishments several times, not to mention the twenty thousand plants Wolfe had, with hundreds of varieties. I stood to one side and watched Wolfe's face. He mumbled something to himself, and then just stood and looked, with his expanse of face five inches from the glass of the case. His emotions didn't show, but from the twitching of a muscle on his neck I knew he was boiling inside. For a quarter of an hour he didn't budge, not even when women bumped against him trying to get a peek at the orchids, though ordinarily he hates to have anyone touching him. Then he backed away and I thought he was through.

"It's hot in here," he said, and was taking off his overcoat. I took it to hold for him.

"Ah, Mr. Wolfe," a voice said. "This is indeed a compliment! What do you think of them?"

It was Lewis Hewitt. Wolfe shook hands with him. He had on another hat and topcoat and gloves, but the same walking stick as the day before—a golden-yellow Malacca with reddish-brown mottles. Any good appraiser would have said $830 as is, on the hoof. He was tall enough to look down at Wolfe with a democratic smile below his aristocratic nose.

"They're interesting," Wolfe said.

Interesting. Ha ha.

"Aren't they marvelous?" Hewitt beamed. "If I had time I'd take one from the case so you could have a good look, but I'm on my way upstairs to judge some roses and

I'm already late. Will you be here a little later? Please do?—Hello, Wade. I'm running."

He went. The "Wade" was for a little guy who had come up while he was talking. As this newcomer exchanged greetings with Wolfe I regarded him with interest, for it was no other than W. G. Dill himself, the employer of my future wife. In many ways he was the exact opposite of Lewis Hewitt, for he looked up at Wolfe instead of down, he wore an old brown suit that needed pressing, and his sharp gray eyes gave the impression that they wouldn't know how to beam.

"You probably don't remember me," he was telling Wolfe. "I was at your house one day with Raymond Plehn—"

"I remember. Certainly, Mr. Dill."

"I just saw Plehn downstairs and he told me you were here. I was going to phone you this afternoon. I wonder if you'd do something for me?"

"That depends—"

"I'll explain. Let's step aside away from this jostling." They moved, and I followed suit. "Do you know anything about the Kurume yellows?"

"I've heard of them." Wolfe was frowning but trying to be courteous. "I've read of them in horticultural journals. A disease fatal to broad-leaved evergreens, thought to be fungus. First found two years ago on some Kurume azaleas imported from Japan by Lewis Hewitt. You had some later, I believe, and so did Watson in Massachusetts. Then Updegraff lost his entire plantation, several acres, of what he called rhodaleas."

"You do know about them."

"I remember what I read."

"Did you see my exhibit downstairs?"

"I glanced at it as I passed." Wolfe grimaced. "The crowd.

I came to see these hybrids. That's a fine group of Cypripedium pubescens you have. Very fine. The Fissipes—"

"Did you see the laurel and azaleas?"

"Yes. They look sick."

"They are sick. They're dying. The Kurume yellows. The underside of the leaves shows the typical brown spots. Some scoundrel deliberately infected those plants, and I'd give a good deal to know who it was. I intend to know who it was!"

Wolfe looked sympathetic, and he really was sympathetic. Between plant growers a fatal fungus makes a bond. "It's too bad your exhibit was spoiled," he said. "But why a personal devil? Why a deliberate miscreant?"

"It was."

"Have you evidence?"

"No. Evidence is what I want."

"My dear sir. You are a child beating the stick it tripped on. You had that disease once on your place. A nest of spores in a bit of soil—"

Dill shook his head. "The disease was at my Long Island place. These plants came from my place in New Jersey. The soil could not possibly have become contaminated."

"With fungi almost anything is possible. A tool taken from one place to the other, a pair of gloves—"

"I don't believe it." Dill's voice indicated that nothing was going to make him believe it. "With the care we take. I am convinced it was done deliberately and maliciously, to ruin my exhibit. And I'm going to know who it was. I'll pay you a thousand dollars to find out for me."

Wolfe abandoned the ship. Not physically, but mentally. His face went bland and blank. "I don't believe I could undertake it, Mr. Dill."

"Why not? You're a detective, aren't you? Isn't that your business?"

"It is."

"This is a job for a detective. Isn't it?"

"No."

"Why not?"

"Because you wouldn't walk across the continent to take a swim in the Pacific Ocean. The effort and expense are out of proportion to the object sought. You say you have no evidence. Do you suspect anyone in particular?"

"No. But I absolutely intend—"

I butted in. I said to Wolfe, "I've got to go and judge some brussels sprouts," and I beat it.

I did have a destination in mind, but mostly I wanted to be somewhere else. What with a couple of lucrative cases we had handled since the first of the year, the budget was balanced for months to come, but even so it always gave me the nettles to hear Wolfe turn down a job, and I didn't want to start riding him right there in front of Hewitt's hybrids. To avoid the mob, I opened a door marked PRIVATE and descended a flight of stairs. This part was not open to the public. On the floor below I made my way through a jungle of packing cases and trees and bushes and spraying equipment and so on, and went along a corridor and turned right with it. This stretch of the corridor extended almost the length of the building, but I knew there was an exit halfway. Along the left wall were cluttered more trees and shrubs and paraphernalia, surplus from the exhibits, and along the right wall, which was the partition between the corridor and the main room, were doors with cards on them, all closed, leading into the exhibits themselves from the back. As I passed the one with a card tacked on it saying RUCKER AND DILL, I threw a kiss at it.

Through the door further on I entered the main room. There was even more of a crowd than when Wolfe and I had passed by half an hour earlier. I dodged through the field as far as the rustic scene which had labels on the rope-posts reading UPDEGRAFF NURSERIES, ERIE, PENNA. The exhibits on this side were a series of peninsulas jutting into the main room, with aisles between them extending back to the partition, on which they were based. I skirted the band of spectators taking in the Updegraff arrangement and halted beside a runty specimen who was standing there by the rope scowling at the foliage.

"Hello, Pete," I said.

He nodded and said hello.

I had met Pete day before yesterday. I didn't really like him. In fact I disliked him. His eyes didn't match and that, together with a scar on his nose, made him look unreliable. But he had been hospitable and made me at home around the place.

"Your peonies look nice," I said socially.

Someone tittered on my left and made a remark which probably wasn't intended for my ear but I have good ears. I turned and saw a pair of vintage Helen Hokinsons from Bronxville. I stared and compelled an eye.

"Yes, madam, peonies," I said. "What's a Cymbidium miranda? You don't know. I've known that since I was knee-high to a grasshopper. What's a Phalaenopsis? Do you know?"

"No, I don't, but I know those are rhododendrons. Peonies! Come, Alice."

I watched them waddle off and turned back to Pete. "Excuse me for chasing your audience, but it's none of her business if I prefer to call them peonies. What were you scowling at? Looking for the Kurume yellows?"

His head jerked around at me. "What about the Kurume yellows?" he demanded.

"Nothing. Just conversation. I heard Dill saying his woodland glade has got it and I wondered if it was spreading. You don't need to look at me like that. I haven't got it."

His left eye blinked but the off-color one didn't. "When did you hear Dill say that?"

"Just a while ago."

"So. What I suspected." He stretched himself as high as he could up on his toes, looking in all directions at the throng. "Did you see my boss?"

"No. I just came—"

Pete darted off. Apparently I had started something. But he went off to the left, towards the front, so I didn't follow him. I turned right, past a rose garden and a couple of other exhibits to Rucker and Dill's.

The crowd was about the same as before; it was only a quarter past three and they wouldn't begin surging against the ropes until four o'clock, when Harry would lie down for a nap and Anne would take off her shoes and stockings, positively never seen before at a flower show in the history of the world. I got behind some dames not tall enough to obstruct the view. Mumblety-peg was over, and Harry was making a slingshot and Anne was knitting. What she was working on didn't look as if it might be something I would be able to use, but anyway what I was interested in was her and not her output, which is a normal and healthy attitude during courtship. She sat there on the grass knitting as if there were no one within miles. Harry was nothing like as good an actor as she was. He didn't look at the spectators' faces, and of course he said nothing, since it was all pantomime and neither of them ever spoke, but by movements and glances he gave it away that he was conscious of the audience every minute.

Naturally I was jealous of him, but aside from that he impressed me as a good deal of a wart. He was about my age and he put something on his hair to make it slick. His hair and eyes were dark and he smirked. Also he was cocky. One reason I had picked Anne was that while they were eating lunch Tuesday Harry had put his hand on her arm and she had pulled away, and it wasn't an invitation to try it again. There had been further indications that she was resolved to keep herself innocent and unsullied for me, though of course she had no way of knowing that it was for me until I got a chance to speak to her. I admit her letting Hewitt decorate her with orchids and take her to dinner had been a bitter pill to swallow, but after all I had no right to expect her to be too spiritual to eat, with her legs.

All of a sudden Harry jumped to his feet and yelled, "Hey!"

It was the first word I had ever heard him utter.

Everyone, including me, looked in the direction of his stare.

"You, Updegraff!" Harry yelled. "Get out of that!"

It was the wholesome young man with the serious chin who had been identified for me as Pete's boss, Fred Updegraff, by Pete himself. At the right corner where the exhibit ended at the partition, he had straddled the rope, stretched an arm and snipped off a peony twig or maybe laurel with a pruning shears, picked up the twig, and was making off with it.

"I'll report that!" Harry yelled.

The crowd muttered and ejaculated with indignation, and for a second I thought we might see a lynching as an added attraction for the most dramatic flower show on record, but all that happened was that two women and a man trotted after Updegraff and started remonstrating with him as he kept going. Believe it or not, Anne never looked up and didn't miss a stroke with her needles. A born actress.

My watch said 3:25. It would be over half an hour before the big scene started, and I didn't dare leave Wolfe alone that long in a strange place, so I regretfully dragged myself away. Retracing my steps, I kept an eye out for

Pete, thinking to tell him that his boss had resorted to crime, but he wasn't visible. Taking the corridor again as a short cut, I saw it was inhabited by a sample who didn't strike me as the flower show type, either for backstage or out front. She was standing there not far from the door with the RUCKER AND DILL card on it, a fancy little trick in a gray coat with 14th Street squirrel on the collar, with a little blue hat and a blue leather handbag under her arm, and as I approached she looked at me with an uneasy eye and a doubtful smile.

I asked her, "You lost, sister?"

"No," she said, and the smile got confident. "I'm waiting for someone."

"Me?"

"Nothing like you."

"That's good. It could have been me a week ago, but now I'm booked."

I went on.

Upstairs I found that Wolfe had stayed put, and W. G. Dill was still with him. Apparently the question of tracking down the gazook who had spoiled Dill's exhibit had been settled one way or the other, for they were arguing about inoculated peat and sterile flasks for germination. I sat down on a vacant spot on a bench. After a while Dill departed and Wolfe went back to the glass case and started peering again, and a few minutes later here came Lewis Hewitt, with his topcoat over his arm. He glanced around as if he was looking for something and asked Wolfe:

"Did I leave my stick here?"

"I haven't seen it. Archie?"

"No, sir."

"Damn it," Hewitt said. "I do leave sticks around, but I wouldn't like to lose that one. Well. Do you want to inspect one of those beauties?"

"Very much. Even without an inspection, I'd like to buy one."

"I imagine you would." Hewitt chuckled. "Plehn offered ten thousand for one the other day." He took a key from his pocket and leaned over the case. "I'm afraid I'm going to be regarded as a miser, but I can't bear to let one go."

"I'm not a commercial grower," Wolfe said ingratiatingly. "I'm an amateur like you."

"I know," Hewitt conceded, lifting out one of the pots as if it was made of star bubbles and angels' breath, "but, my dear fellow, I simply couldn't part with one."

From there on the scene was painful. Wolfe was so damn sweet to him I had to turn my head away to conceal my feelings. He flattered him and yessed him and smiled at him until I expected any minute to hear him offer to dust off his shoes, and the worst of it was, it was obvious he wasn't getting anywhere and wasn't going to. When Hewitt went on and on with a discourse about ovules and pollen tubes, Wolfe beamed at him as if he was fascinated and, finally, when Hewitt offered to present him with a couple of C. hassellis, Wolfe thanked him as if they were just what he asked Santa Claus for, though he had twenty specimens as good or better under his own glass. At a quarter past four I began to fidget. Not only would I have liked to give Wolfe a kick in the fundament for being such a sap, but also I wanted to conduct him past the woodland glade and prove to him that he was wrong when he said my affianced was too long from the knees down, and the big scene would end at four thirty, when Anne would flip water out of the pool onto her co-picnicker to wake him from his nap. That always got a big laugh.

So I was relieved when they started off. Ordinarily Wolfe would have had me carry the two pots of C. hassellis, but he toted them himself, one in each hand, to show

Hewitt how precious he thought they were. The big toad-eater. But the worst was yet to come. We went by the back stairs, and, at my suggestion, along the corridor on the floor below, and there on the floor at the base of the door to Rucker and Dill's exhibit, I saw an object I recognized. I halted and told Hewitt:

"There's your cane."

Hewitt stood and looked at it and demanded, "How in the name of heaven did it get there?"

And by gum, Wolfe told me to pick it up for him! I should have resigned on the spot, but I didn't want to make a scene in front of Hewitt, so I stopped and grabbed it. There was a piece of green string looped on the crook and I brushed it off and extended the crook end toward Hewitt, controlling an impulse to jab him in the ribs. He thanked me democratically and we went on.

"Curious," Hewitt said. "I certainly didn't leave it there. Very odd."

A door ahead of us opened and a man emerged. The door had a card on it, UPDEGRAFF NURSERIES, and the man was the twig-snitcher, Fred Updegraff. At sight of us he stopped, and stood there as we went by. A little farther on, after passing two more doors with exhibitors' cards on them, I swerved to one that wasn't labeled and turned the knob and opened it.

"Where are you going?" Wolfe demanded.

"The water nymph. The pool episode. I thought you might—"

"Bosh. That bedlam—"

"It's really worth seeing," Hewitt declared. "Charming. Perfectly charming. Really delightful. I'll come too."

He headed for the door I was holding open, and Wolfe followed him like an orderly after a colonel, his hands full of potted plants. It would have been comical if it hadn't been disgusting. I kept in front so as not to have to look at him.

At the glade the audience was five and six deep around the ropes to the point on either side where the bushes were in the way, but all three of us were tall enough to get a good view. Anne was putting on a swell performance, dabbling with her toes and swishing around. Her knees were beautiful. I was proud of her. Harry was stretched out in the usual spot for his nap, his head on a grassy mound alongside the rocks and bushes, with a newspaper over his face. The audience was chattering. Anne kicked water onto a cluster of flowers that hung over the pool, and glistening drops fell from the petals.

"Charming," Hewitt said.

"Delightful," Wolfe said. "Archie, will you kindly take these plants? Be very careful—"

Pretending not to hear him, I moved off to the right. Partly I thought he needed some ignoring, but also I wanted to get a better look at Harry's right leg and foot. They were twisted into a strange and unnatural position for a man pretending to take a nap. I stretched tiptoe to get a good look over heads and hats and decided that either his shoe hurt him or he was doing a yogi leg exercise, and went back to Anne just as she took another glance at her wrist watch. She swished once more, swung her feet out of the pool, cast a mischievous eye on her companion, reached into the pool with her cupped hand, and sloshed water over Harry's shirt. The audience screeched with glee.

But Harry didn't take his cue. He was supposed to jerk himself up and blink and look mad, but he didn't move. Anne stared at him in astonishment. Someone called:

"Douse him again!"

I had a quick hunch it wasn't funny, with his leg twisted like that. Pushing through to the front, I got over the rope. As I started across the grass a guard yelled at me, and so did some of the spectators, but I kept going and was bent over Harry when the guard grabbed my arm.

"Hey, you—"

"Shut up." I shook him off and lifted the newspaper enough to see Harry's face, and after one glimpse dropped the paper back over it. As I did that I sniffed. I thought I smelled something, a faint something that I recognized.

"What is it? What's the matter?" a voice above me asked.

It was the first time I had ever heard Anne's voice, but I didn't reply or look up at her because I was seeing something about the moss which clung to the face of the rocks just back of Harry's head. On account of the shrubs and rocks I couldn't get around to see the top of his head, so I reached a hand to feel of it, and the end of my finger went right into a hole in his skull, away in, and it was like sticking your finger into a warm apple pie. I pulled away and started wiping my finger off on the grass, and realized with a shock that the two white things there were Anne's bare feet. I nearly got blood on them.

Chapter 3

I stood up and told Anne, "Put on your shoes and stockings."

"What—"

"Do as I tell you." I had the guard by the sleeve and stabbed into his sputtings, "Get a cop." By the way his mouth fell open I saw he was too dumb even for something as simple as that without a fireside chat, so I turned to call to Hewitt and there was Fred Updegraff inside the ropes headed for us. His eyes were on Anne, but when I intercepted him and told him to get a cop he about-faced without a word and went. Wolfe's voice barked above the din:

"What the devil are you doing in there?"

I ignored him again and raised my voice to address the multitude: "Ladies and gentlemen. That's all for today. Mr. Gould has had an attack. If you're sensible you'll go and look at flowers. If you're morbid or have got the itch you'll stay where you are—outside the ropes—"

A flash bulb flared at the left. Sympathetic murmurs arose, but they seemed to be a hundred percent morbid. At the right a guy with a camera came diving under the rope, but that was something for which arrangements had already been made inside the guard's head and he responded promptly and adequately. I was gratified to see that Anne appeared to have a modicum of wits. She must have seen the color of what I had wiped from my finger, but she was sitting on the grass getting her feet shod, hastily but efficiently.

"Archie!" Wolfe's voice came in his most menacing tone. I knew what was eating him. He wanted me to get out of there and drive him home, and he thought I was showing off, and he knew I was sore. As he called my name again I turned my back on him to welcome the law. A big flatfoot with no neck shoved through the crowd to the rope and got over it and strode across the grass. I blocked his way at Harry's feet.

"What's wrong with him?" he asked gruffly.

I moved aside and let him pass. He stopped and got a corner of the newspaper and jerked it off.

"Archie!" Wolfe bellowed.

Some of the spectators could see Harry's face and they were reacting. The ropes were bellied in, taut, with the pressure from behind. The guard was charging across the grass at them and Anne was on her feet again and Fred Updegraff was there.

"Hell, he's dead," the cop said.

"You guessed it," I conceded. "Shall I get some help?"

"Go ahead."

I won't say that I already knew things I didn't know, but I already had stirrings above the ears and, besides, I didn't want Wolfe to bust a lung, so I went that way and found him standing with Hewitt a few paces to the rear of the throng.

"Hold everything," I muttered to him.

"Confound you—"

"I said hold everything." I cantered off to the phone booths at the front of the room, parted with a nickel and dialed a number and got connected with Extension 19, gave my name and asked for Inspector Cramer. His voice came:

"What do you want?"

"Me? Nothing. I'm helping with the chores. Wolfe and I are up at the Flower Show—"

"I'm busy!"

"Okay. Now you're busier. Rucker and Dill's exhibit, third floor, Flower Show. Man murdered. Shot through the top of the head. Lying there on the grass guarded by one bull-necked bull who will never be an inspector. That's all."

"Wait a min—"

"Can't. I'm busy."

I slid out of the booth and dodged through the traffic back across the room. In that short time the mob surrounding the glade had doubled in size. A glance showed me that the cop and the guard had got reinforcements and Anne and Fred Updegraff were not in sight, and Wolfe and Hewitt had retreated to the other side of the rose garden next door. W. G. Dill was with them. Wolfe glared at me as I approached. He was still hanging onto those measly plants and was speechless with rage.

". . . feel a sort of responsibility," Hewitt was saying. "I am Honorary Chairman of the Committee. I don't like to shirk responsibility, but what can I do—just look at them—"

"That policeman," Dill said. "Imbecile. Wouldn't let me in my own exhibit. Broke my shoulder blade. It feels like it." He worked his shoulder up and down, grimacing. "There's the doctor—no—"

"A doctor won't help any. He's dead."

They looked at me. Dill stopped working his shoulder. "Dead? Dead!" He darted off and burrowed into the crowd.

"You said he had an attack," Hewitt regarded me accusingly. "How can he be dead? What did he die of?"

"He ceased breathing."

"Archie," Wolfe said in his most crushing tone. "Stop that. I asked you an hour ago to take these plants. Take them, and take me home."

"Yes, sir." I took the plants. "But I can't leave yet. I'm looking—"

"Good heavens," Hewitt said. "What a calamity . . . poor Dill . . . I must see . . . excuse me . . ." He marched off towards the main stair.

At that instant I caught sight of an object I had been halfway expecting to see. I only got a glimpse of the gray coat with its collar of 14th Street squirrel, for she came from the other side and disappeared into the crowd. I put the pots on the floor at the edge of the rose garden and dashed off before Wolfe could say a word. I didn't care how sore it made him because he had it coming to him after his degrading performance with Hewitt, but I admit I glanced back over my shoulder as I went to see if he was throwing something. His face was purple. I'll bet he lost ten pounds that afternoon.

I skirted the throng and went into it on the other side. In a minute I saw her, squirming through to the front. I took it easy working through to her because I didn't want to make myself conspicuous, and, getting right behind her, saw that the blue leather bag was under her right arm. I shifted Wolfe's coat to my own right arm and under its cover got my fingers on the end of the bag and pulled gently. It started coming, and she was so interested in what she was trying to see around the people still in front of her that she didn't notice it even when the bag was out from under her arm and safely under Wolfe's coat. I kept an eye on her as I backed out, apologizing to the flower lovers as I went, and as soon as I was in the clear turned and made for the stairs.

In the men's room on the second floor I spent a nickel to achieve privacy and sat down and opened the bag, which was monogrammed "RL." It inventoried about as usual, handkerchief and compact and purse and so on, but it also had what I was after, her name and address. They were on an envelope addressed to Miss Rose Lasher, 326 Morrow Street, New York City, which checked with the RL on the bag. I copied it in my notebook. The letter inside was from Ellie and explained why she hadn't paid back the two dollars. And another item was more than I had bargained for. It was a clipping from the *Gazette* of a picture of Harry and Anne playing mumblety-peg. It had cut edges, not torn, and was neatly folded.

I put everything back in, went back to the third floor, worked my way into the crowd, not taking it so easy this time, found her in the front row against the rope, and put my hand on her shoulder. Her head twisted around.

"Will you please—" she began indignantly.

"Okay, sister. It's me. Here's your bag."

"My bag!"

"You dropped it and I risked life and limb to get it. It's yours, isn't it?"

"Sure it's mine!" She grabbed it.

"Say think you."

She mumbled something and was through with me. I glanced at the scene. The cast had been augmented. The contents of two radio police cars, four of them in uniform, were there in the glade, one of them standing at Harry's feet watching a doctor, who was on his knees applying a stethoscope. W. G. Dill stood at the cop's side, his hands in his pockets, scowling. There was no sign that anyone had got interested in the moss on the rocks. I backed out again without bruising anyone seriously and circled around to the rose garden to rejoin Wolfe.

He wasn't there.

He was gone. The two pots were there on the floor, but he wasn't anywhere.

The damn hippopotamus, I thought. He'll get lost. He'll be kidnapped. He'll fall in a hole. He'll catch cold.

I went back down to the men's room on the second floor and yelled his name in front of the private apartments, but no soap. I went up to the fourth, to the orchid benches. No. I went down to the ground floor and out the main exit and to where I had parked the car on 46th Street, but he wasn't in it. It was trying to snow in March gusts. I spat at a snowflake as it sailed by. Our little Nero, I thought, out on such a night and no coat. The bag fat flumpus. I'll put salt on his grapefruit. It was a quarter past five.

I stood and applied logic to it. Had he taken a taxi home? Not the way he hated taxis. What, as I had left him standing there, what had been his most burning desires? That was easy. To shoot me, to sit down, and to drink beer. He couldn't shoot me because I wasn't there. Where might he have found a chair?

I went back and paid four bits to get in again, mounted one flight, and made my way across the grain of the traffic to the corner of the room where a door said OFFICE. People were standing around, and one of them plucked at my sleeve as I put my hand on the knob, and I recognized him. It was the gray-haired geezer I had seen on previous days looking at Anne from a distance as if he was saying his prayers. He looked worried under an old felt hat, and his fingers on my sleeve were trembling.

"Please," he said, "if you're going in there will you please give this to Miss Anne Tracy?"

"Is she in there?"

"Yes, she went in—I saw her go in—"

I took the folded piece of paper and said I'd see that Miss Tracy got it, opened the door and entered, and was in an anteroom containing a tired-looking woman at a desk. I smiled at her irresistibly to keep her quiet, unfolded the piece of paper, and read what it said.

Dear daughter,

I hope there is no serious trouble. I am outside here. If there is anything I can do let me know.

Your father.

It was written with a pencil on cheap white paper. I folded it up again, thinking that one of the first jobs to tackle would be to buy my father-in-law a new hat.

"Do you want something?" the woman at the desk asked in a sad and skeptical tone. I told her I had an important message for Miss Anne Tracy, and she opened her mouth and then decided not to use it any more and motioned to one of three doors. I opened it and passed through, and the first thing I saw was Nero Wolfe sitting in a chair almost big enough for him, with a tray on a table beside him holding four beer bottles, and a glass in his hand.

You can't beat logic.

On another chair right in front of him, facing him, was Anne. Propped against a desk at the left was Lewis Hewitt. A man I didn't know was at another desk writing something, and another one was standing by a window with Fred Updegraff.

Wolfe saw me enter. I saw him see me. But he went on talking to Anne without dropping a stitch:

". . . a matter of nerves, yes, but primarily it depends on oxygenation of the blood. The most remarkable case of self-control I ever saw was in Albania in 1915, displayed by a donkey, I mean a four-legged donkey, which toppled over a cliff—"

I was standing by him. "Excuse me," I said icily. "For you, Miss Tracy." I extended the paper.

She looked up at me, looked at the paper, took it, unfolded it, and read it.

"Oh," she said. She glanced around and looked up at me again. "Where is he?"

"Outside."

"But I . . ." Her brow wrinkled. "Would you tell him . . . no . . . I'll go . . ."

She got up and started for the door. I went to open it for her, saw that Hewitt had the same intention, quickened my step, beat him to the knob, and swung it open. Anne was walking through, and then she wasn't. A man barging through from the other side ran smack into her and nearly knocked her over, and I grabbed her arm to help her get her balance. I beat Hewitt to that too.

"Pardon me," the intruder said. His eyes swept the room and everything in it and went back to Anne. "Are you Anne Tracy?"

"She is Miss Anne Tracy," Hewitt said, "and that is scarcely the way—"

Anne was sidling by to get to the door. The man put an arm out to stop her.

"Where are you going?"

"I'm going to see my father."

"Where is he?"

Another arm got in on it. Fred Updegraff arrived and his hand came out and contacted the intruder's ribs and gave a healthy shove.

"Learn some manners," he said gruffly. "What business is—"

"Permit me," I interposed. "This is Inspector Cramer

of the Homicide Squad." I indicated another man on the door sill. "And Sergeant Purley Stebbins."

"Even so," Lewis Hewitt said in a tone of displeasure. "It is scarcely necessary to restrain Miss Tracy by force. She merely wishes to speak with her father. I am Lewis Hewitt, Inspector. May I ask—"

"Where is your father?"

"Just outside the door," I said.

"Go with her, Purley. All right, Miss Tracy. Come back in here, please."

Purley went out at her heels. That cleared the doorway for another man to enter, W. G. Dill. His lips were in a thinner line than ever, and without looking at anybody or saying anything he crossed to a chair by the rear wall and sat down.

"Hello, Wolfe," Cramer said.

"How do you do, Inspector." With only two grunts, one under par, Wolfe got to his feet and moved forward. "Come, Archie. We'll only be in the way."

"No," Cramer said meaningly.

"No?" Wolfe halted. "No what?"

"Goodwin won't be in the way. On the contrary. At least until I get through with him."

"He's going to drive me home."

"Not now he isn't."

"May I ask what this is all about?" Hewitt was still displeased. "This surveillance of Miss Tracy? This attitude—"

"Certainly, Mr. Hewitt. Sit down." Cramer waved at chairs, of which there were plenty. "Everybody sit down. This is going to be—ah, Miss Tracy, did you find your father? Good. Pull that chair around for Miss Tracy, Purley. Sit down, Goodwin."

I attended to the chair for Anne myself, then turned to face the Inspector.

"No, thanks. I'm nervous."

"You are," Cramer growled. "The day you're nervous I'll shave with a butter knife. How did you know that man had been shot in the top of the head when you called me on the phone?"

Some of them made noises, but Anne didn't. Her head jerked up and her nostrils tightened, but that was all. I admired her more all the time. Hewitt exclaimed, "Shot!" and Fred Updegraff demanded, "What man?"

"Harry Gould," I told him. I grinned at Cramer. "As you see, I didn't blab around. I saved it for you—"

"How did you know?"

"Good heavens," Hewitt said blankly. He rose half out of his chair and then dropped back again.

"It was nothing to write home about," I said. "I looked at his face and he looked dead. I smelled cordite. I saw a jagged hole in the moss at the back of his head, and the moss was puffed out. I couldn't see the top of his head from where I was, but I felt of it, and my finger went in a hole. By the way, don't build a theory from some blood on the grass about where his knees were. I wiped my finger there."

I saw Anne gulp.

"Confound you," Wolfe said angrily, "I might have known."

"Why did you go to him in the first place?" Cramer demanded. "You climbed the ropes and ran to him. Why did you do that?"

"Because he didn't move when Miss Tracy threw water on him, and because I had already noticed that his leg and foot were twisted in an unnatural position."

"Why did you notice that?"

"Ah," I said, "now you've got me. I give up. I'm trapped. Why does anybody notice anything?"

"Especially a nervous man like you," he said sarcastically. "What were you doing there? Why did you come here?"

"I brought Mr. Wolfe."

"Did he come here on a case?"

"You know damn well he didn't. He never goes anywhere on a case. He came to look at flowers."

"Why were you there at that particular exhibit?"

"For the same reason that other people were. To watch Miss Tracy dabble her feet in the pool."

"Did you know Miss Tracy? Or Gould?"

"No."

"Did you, Wolfe?"

"No," Wolfe said.

Cramer resumed with me. "And smelling the cordite and seeing the hole in the moss and feeling the one in his head, how did you figure someone had shot him? By lying hidden in the bushes and aiming through a crack in the rocks?"

"Now have a heart, Inspector." I grinned at him. "If you're not careful you'll trap me again. At the moment I didn't do much figuring, but that was over an hour ago and you know what my brain is when it gets started. Gould took his nap at the same hour each day, and he put his head in exactly the same spot—"

"How do you know that?"

"Mr. Wolfe has been sending me here to look at orchids. That's a matter I'd rather not dwell on. The pile of rocks was only eight or nine inches from his head. Place a gun among the rocks at the right height, wedge it in, aimed the right way, and replace the moss. The rocks and the moss would muffle the report so that no one would notice it in that big noisy room—or what if they did notice it? Fasten a string to the trigger—make it green string so it won't be seen among the foliage. At the proper time, which will be anywhere between four and four thirty, pull the string."

"Pull the string how? From where?"

"Oh, suit yourself." I waved a hand. "Hide in the bushes and after you've pulled it sneak out the door at the back of the exhibit that leads to the corridor. Or if the string's long enough, run it through the crack at the bottom of the door and then you can pull it from the corridor, which would be safer. Or if you want to be fancy, tie the string to the doorknob and it will be pulled by whoever opens the door from the corridor side. Or if you want to be still fancier, run the string around the trunk of a bush and have its end a loop dangling into the pool, and take off your shoes and stockings and swish your feet around in the pool, and catch the loop with your toes and give it a jerk, and who would ever suspect—"

"That's a lie!"

That blurted insult came from Fred Updegraff. He confronted me, and his chin was not only serious, it was bigoted, and anyone might have thought I was a caterpillar eating his best peony.

"Nonsense!" came another blurt, from W. G. Dill, who didn't leave his chair.

"It seems to me—" Lewis Hewitt began sarcastically.

"Pooh," I said. "You cavaliers. I wouldn't harm a hair of her head. Don't you suppose the Inspector had thought of that? I know how his mind works—"

"Can it," Cramer growled. "The way your mind works." His eyes were narrowed at me. "We'll discuss that a little later, when I'm through with Miss Tracy. The gun was wedged among the rocks and covered with the moss, and the string was tied to the trigger, and the string was green, so you're quite a guesser—"

"How long was the string?"

"Long enough to reach. What else do you know?"

I shook my head. "If you can't tell guessing from logic—"

"What else do you know?"

"Nothing at present."

"We'll see." Cramer looked around. "If there's a room where I can go with Miss Tracy—"

The man who had been writing at a desk stood up. "Certainly, Inspector. That door there—"

"Who are you?"

"I'm Jim Hawley of the house staff. I don't think there's anyone in there—I'll see—"

But there was an interruption. The door to the anteroom opened, and in came a delegation of four. In front was a dick whom I recognized as a member of the squad, next came a lady, next my friend Pete with unmatched eyes, and bringing up the rear a cop in uniform. The lady wore a gray coat with a squirrel collar and had a blue leather bag under her arm, but I didn't presume on old acquaintance by speaking to her.

Chapter 4

Cramer took in the influx with a glance and asked, "What have you got, Murphy?"

"Yes, sir." The dick stood with his shoulders straight. He was the military type. "At or about half past four o'clock this young woman was seen in the corridor opening the door leading to the Rucker and Dill exhibit."

"Who saw her?"

"I did," Pete spoke up.

"Who are you?"

"I am Pete Arango. I work for Updegraff Nurseries. That's my boss there, Mr. Updegraff. I went through the door at the back of our exhibit, into the corridor, to get some cookies, and I—"

"To get what?"

"Cookies. I eat cookies. In my locker in the corridor."

"Okay. You eat cookies. And saw what?"

"I saw her opening that door. Rucker and Dill. After all what happened I remembered it and I told a cop—"

"Did she go inside?"

Pete shook his head. "She saw me and she shut the door."

"Did she say anything?"

"No, she didn't have anything to say."

"Did you?"

"No, I went to my locker and got the cookies, and she must have gone away because when I came back she wasn't there. Then when I got back on the floor and saw—"

Cramer turned to the young woman. "What's your name?"

"None of your business!" she snapped.

"Yes, sir," the dick said. "She won't co-operate."

"What do you mean, I won't co-operate?" She was indignant, but I wouldn't have said she looked scared. "I admit I opened the door and looked in, don't I? I got into the corridor by mistake and I was looking for a way out. And why should I have to tell you my name and get my name in the papers—"

"Why didn't you get out the way you got in?"

"Because I got in away around at the other side, and I just thought . . . hey! Hello there!"

Everyone looked the way she was looking, which resulted in all of us looking at Fred Updegraff. Fred himself turned red and was turning redder, as he met her gaze.

"Well," he said, and seemed to think he had said something.

"It was you," she said, "there with the door open, stooping down there peeking in when you heard me."

"Sure," Fred acknowledged, "sure it was me."

"The Rucker and Dill door?" Cramer demanded.

"Yes."

"Were you looking for a way out too?"

"No."

"What were you looking for?"

"I was—" Fred swallowed it. He looked red and flustered, and then all of a sudden he looked relieved. There was no telling what sort of idea had popped into his head that relieved him and pleased him so much, but he certainly showed it. He spoke louder as if he didn't want anyone to miss it: "I was looking at Miss Tracy. I've been doing that all week. My name is Fred Updegraff and I'm an exhibitor here. I was looking at Miss Tracy!" It sounded as if he almost thought he was singing it.

Cramer was unimpressed. "I'll have a talk with you later, Mr. Updegraff." He turned to the Sergeant. "Purley, you stay here with Mr. Updegraff and Goodwin and this young woman and this man Pete. Murphy, come with me and Miss Tracy. The rest of you can go if you want—"

"Just a minute." Hewitt, who hadn't sat down again, moved a step. "I am Lewis Hewitt."

"So I understand," Cramer grunted.

"And I have responsibilities here as the Honorary Chairman of the Committee. Without any wish to interfere with the performance of your duties, I feel that Miss Tracy, who is only a young girl, should properly be protected from any undue annoyance or unpleasantness—"

"Allow me, Hewitt," W. G. Dill had got up and walked over. He faced Cramer. "I'm Miss Tracy's employer and I suppose I ought to look after her. If you don't mind I'll go along with her."

I was keeping tabs on Anne, knowing that the best time to get the lowdown on a woman is when she's under stress. I thought she was doing fine. After four straight days in a glaring spotlight as the star attraction of a flower show, with such by-products as having her picture taken with Billy Rose and dining out with Lewis Hewitt, here she was kerplunk in the mire with murder-mud ready to splatter all over her, and so far she had done nothing to forfeit my respect, even when I had explained how you could pull a trigger with your toes. But at this juncture she wasn't so hot. She might have spoken up with something suitable about being armored in her virtue and not needing to be looked after by any sourpuss employer or millionaire orchid fancier, but all she did was deadpan W. G. Dill without opening her trap. I began to suspect she either had depths I hadn't plumbed or was a bit limited in the mental area—but don't get me wrong, I was still faithful. Even as a deadpan, the sight of her face—for the mental side of life you can go to the library.

She went off with Cramer. Cramer informed both Hewitt and Dill that it wasn't necessary for them to protect her against annoyance, and took her and Murphy through the door that had been indicated to an inner room. But not without another brief delay.

"Mr. Cramer! If you please?"

It was Nero Wolfe speaking. I concealed a grin. Of course he was going to request, or demand, depending on which he thought would work best, that I be allowed to drive him home. I hope Cramer would say yes. Then, after we got in the sedan and he started raving, I would let him rave, and when he was through I would stick my little dagger in his ribs and give it a twist. It wasn't often I had a chance like that.

Cramer had turned. "What do you want?"

"I want," Wolfe said, "to finish a discussion I was having with Mr. Hewitt about orchids."

"Go ahead—"

"And not in a menagerie. In decent privacy. We can find a room somewhere."

"Go ahead. I said the rest of you could go—"

"And Mr. Goodwin must be present to take notes. He will be available when you want him. You can't legally detain him, anyhow, unless you are prepared—"

Cramer snorted in exasperation. "Oh, for God's sake. Discuss orchids. All I want is Goodwin when I want him."

He crossed the sill with the other two, and the door was closed behind them. I glared at Wolfe without any attempt to cover it, and Purley Stebbins gazed at him suspiciously. Neither of us was making any impression on Wolfe, who had got up from his chair and was speaking to Lewis Hewitt in an undertone. Hewitt, frowning, nodded without enthusiasm, and moved toward the door to the anteroom with Wolfe at his heels.

"Come, Archie," Wolfe said.

Purley blocked me. "Where you going?"

"The other end of the anteroom," Hewitt said. "A room there."

Purley hated it. He did hate it. Me detained and going through doors like that. He didn't even smile when I playfully stuck a thumb in his ribs as I went by.

The room at the other end of the anteroom wasn't much more than a cubbyhole, with one window, a couple of small wooden tables, and four wooden chairs. The sad woman in the anteroom came in and turned on the light and went out again and closed the door. Wolfe scowled at the skimpy chairs and darted a glance at me, but I ignored it because I was in no mood to lug in the comfortable seat he had left in the other room. He compressed his lips and sat down, taking care to center himself on what seat there was.

"Sit down, Mr. Hewitt," he invited.

Hewitt stood. "This is an odd performance." He looked at me and back at Wolfe. "What you can possibly have to say to me so confidential as to require—"

"I have," Wolfe said brusquely. "I assure you."

"About orchids? That seems hardly—"

"Not orchids. Murder. I know who shot that man."

Hewitt's eyes opened wide. "You know who shot him?"

"I do."

"But my dear Mr. Wolfe." Hewitt was displeased but courteous. "That is scarcely a matter to discuss confidentially with me. The proper authorities—"

"I prefer to discuss it with you first. I suggest that we

keep our voices as low as possible. It's quite possible that a policeman has his ear at the door—"

"Bosh! This melodramatic—"

"Please, Mr. Hewitt. Don't sneer at melodrama; that's only a point of view. I wish to give you a fresh point of view on the death of Harry Gould. The shot was fired by my assistant, Mr. Goodwin. —Please let me finish. First to establish the fact. Archie?"

I had sat down. The fat bum had taken my dagger away from me. I looked at him and said bitterly, "What if I let you down?"

"You won't. Anyway, you can't. I saw the piece of string you brushed off of it. And I wish to say that your performance this afternoon has been satisfactory. Completely satisfactory throughout. Was there a tug when you picked it up? That's the only detail I lack."

"What the devil is all this?" Hewitt demanded without courtesy. "If you actually—"

"Please, Mr. Hewitt. And keep your voice down. I'll state the situation as briefly as possible. Should I report it to Mr. Cramer—"

"There was a tug," I said. "A little jerk. I didn't especially notice it at the time because I was sore as hell."

Wolfe nodded. "I know you were. My report to Mr. Cramer would be this: that Lewis Hewitt said he had lost his cane. A little later, in the corridor on the third floor, we saw the cane lying on the floor with its crook against the crack under the door leading to the Rucker and Dill exhibit. That was at twenty minutes past four. Mr. Goodwin picked up the cane, and as he did so felt a tug. He calls it a little jerk, but he is exceptionally strong and was in a savage emotional state. Looped on the crook of the cane was a piece of green string which he brushed off before he handed it to its owner."

"I saw no string," Hewitt snapped.

"Maybe not," Wolfe admitted. "People who inherit wealth don't have to bother to see things. But certainly Mr. Goodwin saw it, and so did I, and he felt the tug. The tug was unquestionably the pulling of the trigger and the breaking of the string. That would be my report to Mr. Cramer, since those are the facts."

"I tell you I saw no string!"

"But we did. Keep your voice down, Mr. Hewitt. And Mr. Goodwin touched it. Surely you don't suppose we cooked this up?"

"I don't—" Hewitt looked at the door, and then at me, and then back at Wolfe. "No. I don't suppose you did. But it's inconceivable—" He stopped and stared. "What's that?"

"The piece of string," Wolfe said.

The son of a gun had pulled it out of his vest pocket. I got up for a look, and it was it. I said, "Good here," and sat down. Hewitt sat down too. He looked as if he had to do something and that was all he could think of.

"You and Mr. Dill and Mr. Goodwin left me there," Wolfe said. "Standing there alone. He left those plants there on the floor—and by the way, I have better hassellis than those, much better, my own growing. At a certain point my head began to work, which was remarkable under the circumstances. I don't say that I foresaw this moment precisely, but I saw enough to impel me to go to the corridor and find this piece of string on the floor and pick it up. It is indubitably the piece that was looped on the crook of your cane. By comparing it with the piece left attached to the trigger, Mr. Cramer can establish our surmise as a certainty. That is, he can if I let him have it. Do you think I should do that?"

"Good heavens," Hewitt muttered. "My stick. Good heavens, do you realize—*my* stick!"

"Exactly," Wolfe agreed. "Don't talk so loud. I do

realize. Whoever rigged up that affair made a loop at the end of the string that could be passed under the door. It may have been an afterthought, ad libbing, suggested by the sight of your cane where you had left it, to pass the loop over the cane and leave it lying there for the first passer-by to pick up. If that hadn't happened before half past four I imagine he would have attended to it himself. I do realize what a story that will be for the newspapers. I doubt if it would lead to any official suspicion that you rigged it up yourself, but the public mind—at least some of it—is even less subtle than Mr. Crammer's."

"Good heavens," Hewitt moaned. "This . . ." He clenched his fingers, and released them, and clenched them again. "This is horrible."

"Oh, I wouldn't say horrible. Disagreeable."

"Horrible. For me. For a Hewitt. Horrible!"

"Perhaps for a Hewitt," Wolfe conceded. "Then all the more reason why this may interest you. I want those orchid plants. All three of them."

That changed things entirely. The change, showing itself on Hewitt's face, took perhaps two seconds all told. Up to then nothing had been threatened but his peace of mind or maybe his reputation, at most his life and liberty. But this was something else again; this threatened his property. It put stone in his heart and steel in his jaw. He eyed Wolfe with a shrewd and stubborn stare.

"I see," he hissed. "So that's it. To put it plainly, blackmail. Blackmail! No! I won't do it!"

Wolfe sighed. "You won't?"

"No!"

"Very well. Then I won't get the orchids, but I'll be saved a lot of trouble. Archie, get Mr. Cramer in here. Tell him it's urgent. I'll not perch on this confounded milking stool any longer than I have to."

I arose and started for the door, not hastily. I knew it

was in the bag because Hewitt hadn't raised his voice. It was only a war of nerves.

"Blackmail," Hewitt said through his teeth.

"Go on, Archie," Wolfe said. I put my hand on the knob.

"Wait a minute," Hewitt said. I turned my head but kept my hand on the knob.

"One of them," Hewitt said. "Select any one."

I went back and sat down.

Wolfe sighed and shook his head. "All three. I won't haggle. I'm going to have to work for them. You may call it blackmail to relieve your feelings, but what about me? It's possible that this evidence I'm withholding from Mr. Cramer is vital evidence, and I don't intend to shield a murderer. If I withhold it I'll have to find the murderer myself, and enough evidence to convict him without this. And if I fail I'll have to tell Mr. Cramer all about it, which would be deplorable, and shall have to return the plants to you, which would be unthinkable. So I shan't fail."

"Two of them," Hewitt said. "Two plants. To be delivered to you when you have satisfactorily performed your part of the bargain." He may have inherited it, but he certainly knew how to hang onto it.

"No," Wolfe said. "All three, and I take them home with me now. You can trust me, I can't trust you, because if it turns out that you killed the man yourself and I get you for it, I'd never get them."

"Do you—" Hewitt was goggle-eyed. "You have the effrontery—you dare to suggest—"

"Not at all. I suggest nothing. I consider contingencies, and I'd be a fool if I didn't." Wolfe put a hand on the edge of the table for leverage and lifted himself from the milking stool. "I'm going home where there is a chair to sit on, and go to work. If you'll please take Mr. Goodwin upstairs and give him the plants so I can take them with me . . ."

Chapter 5

Of course I had a card up my sleeve. Wolfe had taken my dagger away and done the twisting himself in Hewitt's ribs instead of his own, but I still had a card.

I had a chance to make arrangements for playing it while Wolfe went around, after we returned to the other room, inviting people to lunch. That was actually what he did. Anyhow he invited W. G. Dill and Fred Updegraff; I heard that much. Apparently he intended to spend the evening thinking it out, and have them all to lunch the next day to announce the result. Hewitt declined my help on the orchid portage from upstairs. It seemed as if he didn't like me. When Wolfe had finished the inviting he calmly opened, without knocking, the door into the room where Cramer had gone with Anne, and disappeared within.

I approached Purley Stebbins, stationed on a chair near the door to the anteroom, and grinned at him reassuringly. He was always upset in the presence of either Wolfe or me, and the two of us together absolutely gave him the fidgets. He gave me a glancing eye and let out a growl.

"Look, Purley," I said cordially, "here's one for the notebook. That lady over there." She was sitting by the far wall with her coat still on and the blue leather bag under her arm. "She's a phony. She's really a Chinese spy. So am I. We were sent to do this job by Hoo Flung Dung. If you don't believe it watch us talk code."

"Go to hell," Purley suggested.

"Yeah? You watch."

I ambled across the room and stood right in front of her so Purley couldn't see her face.

"Hello, dear old friend," I said not too loud.

"You've got a nerve," she said. "Beat it."

"Nerve? Me?"

"Beat it. 'Dear old friend!' I never saw you before."

"Aha!" I smiled down at her. "Not a chance in the world. If I tell them I saw you in that corridor at half past three waiting for someone, they'll believe me, don't think they won't, and you'll have to start all over again about opening that door at half past four because you got there by mistake and were looking for a way out. Think fast and don't tell me to beat it again or we part forever. And control your face and keep your voice down."

Her fingers were twisting under a fold of the coat. "What do you want?"

"I want to get to know you better. I'll be leaving here in a minute to drive my boss home, but I'll be back before long for a little talk with the Inspector. Then I'll go to the news movie in Grand Central and you'll be there in the back row. Won't you?"

"Yes."

"You're sure."

"Yes."

"You'd better be. If you are, it's all right that you never saw me before. If you put over your song and dance there may be a tail on you when you leave. Don't try to shake him. We'll take care of that when we leave the movie. Understand?"

"Yes."

"Righto. Stick to me and you'll wear black orchids."

I started to go back to Purley to kid him out of any suspicions that might be pecking at the shell, but a door opened and Wolfe emerged, and Cramer stood on the sill and spoke:

"Purley! Goodwin's taking Wolfe home and will be back in half an hour."

"Yeah," Purley said disrespectfully.

"Come, Archie," Wolfe said.

We waited in the anteroom, and in a few minutes here came Lewis Hewitt, followed by a guard balancing the glass case on his upper limbs. The transfer was made to me without ceremony, after Wolfe peered through the glass for a good gloating look, and off we went. When we got to where I had parked the car Wolfe got in the back, always a major operation, and I deposited the case on the floor at his feet. Ten minutes later we arrived at the old house on West 35th Street near the river, and the sigh he heaved as he deposited his weight and volume in a chair that had been made for them was a record for both depth and duration.

"You'd better get back up there," he said. "I regret it and I resent it, but I gave Mr. Cramer my word. Theodore will attend to the plants. Get back for dinner if you can. We're having saucisse minuit."

He was being sweet. "I didn't give Cramer my word," I suggested.

"No." He wiggled a finger at me. "Archie! No shenanigan."

"I'll see. But I need refreshment."

I went to the kitchen and put two bowls of crackers and milk where they belonged, meanwhile chinning with Fritz and getting sniffs of the sausage he was preparing. Eating crackers and milk and smelling saucisse minuit simultaneously is like sitting with your arm around a country lass while watching Hedy Lamarr raise the temperature. I told Fritz to save some for me if I was late getting back, and departed.

It was 7:15 when I entered the big inside room of the offices on the second floor of Grand Central Palace. There were a dozen or more people in there, most of whom were new to me, but including W. G. Dill and Lewis Hewitt. Updegraff wasn't in sight, and neither was Anne Tracy, and neither was the girl friend I had a date with. Her absence made it desirable to get troublesome without delay, but it wasn't necessary because in a couple of minutes the door to the inner room opened and Pete Arango came out, and I got a sign from Purley and went in. Cramer was there with a dick I had never seen and Murphy with a notebook. His unlighted cigar was chewed halfway to the end and he looked unjubilant.

"Now," I said brightly, taking a seat, "what can I do to help?"

"Join a circus," Cramer said. "By God, you'll clown at your own funeral. What have you been hanging around here all week for?"

That was all it amounted to, a bunch of whats and whys and whens and four pages of the notebook filled, and my wit wasted on the homicide squad as usual. As a matter of fact, the wit was below par because I wanted to get out of there for my date, since it appeared that she had had her session and been turned loose. So I kept it fairly succinct and tried to co-operate on details, and we were about running out of material when the door opened and in came an undersized dick with a flat nose. Cramer looked at him and demanded:

"What the hell are you doing back here?"

The dick's mouth opened and shut again. It didn't want to say what it had to say. On the second try it got it out:

"I lost her."

Cramer groaned and looked speechless.

"It wasn't my fault," the dick said, "I swear it wasn't, Inspector. That damn subway. A local rolled in and stopped and she hung back like waiting for an express and then the last second she dived through—"

"Can it," Cramer said. "Choke on it. My God. The wonder to me is that—what does it matter what the wonder to me is? What's that name and address?"

Murphy flipped back through the pages of his notebook and stopped at one. "Ruby Lawson. One fourteen Sullivan Street."

The dick got out his memo book and wrote it down. "I don't think it was deliberate," he said. "I think she just changed her mind. I think she just—"

"You think? You say you think?"

"Yes, Inspector, I—"

"Get out. Take another man, take Dorsey, and go to that address and look into her. Don't pick her up. Keep on her. And for God's sake don't think. It's repulsive, the idea of you thinking."

The thinker made himself scarce. Naturally I was now itching to be on my way, so I leaned back comfortably and crossed my legs and began, "You know, when I am tailing someone and they go into a subway station, it is my invariable custom—"

"You can go," Cramer snapped. "On out. If I want you, which God forbid, I know where to get you."

"But I think—"

"I said go!"

I got up leisurely and went out leisurely, and on my way through the outer room paused for a friendly word with Purley, but when I got to the stairs outside I stepped on it. It was at least a hundred to one that I had been stood up, but nevertheless I hotfooted it to the Lexington Avenue entrance of Grand Central Station and on to the newsreel theater, parted with money, and entered. She wasn't in the back row, and I didn't waste time inspecting any other rows. Since she had given a phony name and address to Cramer, and had been smart enough to make it one that matched the RL on her bag, I figured she probably wouldn't be letting grass come up between her toes. Out in the lighted corridor I took a hasty glance at a page in my memo book, considered patronizing the subway and decided no, and headed for 46th Street where I had parked the car.

My high-hatting the subway nearly lost me a trick, for it was slow work at that hour getting around on to Park Avenue, but once headed downtown I made good time.

Number 326 Morrow Street, down at the southern fringe of Greenwich Village, was one of those painted brick fronts that were painted too long ago. There were supposed to be two lights on black iron brackets at the entrance to the vestibule, but only one was working. I parked across the street and moseyed over. Inside the vestibule was the usual row of mailboxes and bell pushes, and the card below one of them had LASHER printed on it. That was okay, but what made it interesting was that on the same card, above LASHER, another name was printed: GOULD. I was leaning over looking at it when the inside door opened and there she was.

It was easy to see that high-hatting the subway had nearly cost me a trick, because she had a traveling bag in her hand and was stooping to pick up a suitcase with the hand she had used to open the door with.

"Allow me," I said, extending a hand. "That looks heavy."

She gave me one startled glance and dropped the suitcase and sat down on it and started to cry. She didn't cover her face with her hands or anything like that, she just burst.

I waited a minute for a lull. "Look," I said, "you're blocking the way in case anyone wants to come in or go out. Let's take these things—"

"You dirty—" The crying interfered with it. "You lousy—"

"No," I said firmly. "No, sister. You stood me up. You humiliated me." I picked up the traveling bag which she had also dropped. "Let's go."

"He's dead," she said. She wasn't bothering about small things like tears. "He's dead, ain't he? Hasn't anybody got any heart at all? The way I had to sit up there—sit there and pretend—" She stopped and chewed her lip, and all of a sudden she stood up and blazed at me. "Who are you, anyway? How did you know who I was? How did you get here so quick? You're a detective, that's what you are, you're a lousy detective—"

"No." I gripped her arm. "If you mean a city employee, no. My name is Archie Goodwin and I work for Nero Wolfe. My car's outside and I'm taking you up to Wolfe's place for a little conference. He's got one of the biggest hearts in the world, encased in a ton of blubber."

Of course she balked. She even defied me to call a cop, but then she started to cry again, and during that deluge I picked up the bag and suitcase and herded her out and across the street to the car. All the way up to 35th Street she cried and I had to lend her a handkerchief.

With my hands full of luggage, I had her precede me up the stoop and ring the bell for Fritz to let us in. He did so, and helped her off with her coat like a head waiter helping the Duchess of Windsor, one of the nicest things about Fritz being that to him anything in a skirt is a lady.

"Mr. Wolfe is at dinner," he announced.

"I'll bet he is. Take Miss Lasher to the office."

I took the luggage with me to the dining room, set it down against the wall, and approached the table. There he was, floating in clouds of bliss. He looked from the luggage to me.

"What's that? Those aren't your bags."

"No, sir," I agreed. "They are the property of an object I brought with me named Rose Lasher, who may help you hang onto those orchids. She is bereaved and hungry and I'm hungry. Shall I stay with her in the office—"

"Hungry? Bring her in here. There's plenty."

I went to the office and returned with her. She had stopped crying but sure was forlorn.

"Miss Lasher," I said, "this is Nero Wolfe. He never discusses business at the table, so we'll eat first and go into things later." I held a chair for her.

"I don't want to eat," she said in a thin voice. "I can't eat."

She ate seven sausages, which was nothing against her grief. Fritz's saucisse minuit would make Gandhi a gourmet.

Chapter 6

"And now," Wolfe demanded, "what is Miss Lasher here for?"

Dinner was over and we were settled in the office. Wolfe was seated behind his desk, leaning back with his fingers laced over his sausage mausoleum, his eyes half closed. I was at my desk, and Rose was in a red leather chair facing Wolfe. The set of her lips didn't indicate that the meal had made her one of us.

I recited particulars, briefly but completely.

"Indeed." Wolfe inclined his head a sixteenth of an inch. "Satisfactory, Archie." The head turned. "You must have a lot to tell, Miss Lasher. Tell it, please."

She looked sullen. "Tell what?"

"Start at the end. Where did you hide in that corridor from half past three to half past four and who and what did you see?"

"I didn't hide. I went out and went back and the second time I saw that man opening that door. Then I went—"

"No. That won't do. You were waiting to intercept Mr. Gould when he came out, and you hid. The police won't like it that you lied to them and gave them a false name and address and were running away. So I may not tell the police if you tell me the truth."

"I wasn't running away. I was merely going to visit a friend."

It was certainly a job to steam her off the envelope. She stuck for ten minutes in spite of all Wolfe said, and she didn't loosen up until after I brought the luggage from the dining room and went through it. I had to dig the keys out of her handbag, and at one point I thought she was going to start clawing and kicking, but finally she stopped squealing and only sat in the chair and made holes in me with her eyes.

I did it thoroughly and methodically. When I got through, the suitcase was nearly filled with female garments and accessories, mostly intimate, and piled on Wolfe's desk was a miscellaneous collection not so female. Shirts and ties, three photographs of Harry Gould, a bunch of snapshots, a bundle of letters tied with string, the top one addressed to Rose, various other items, among them a large Manila envelope fastened with a clasp.

I opened the envelope and extracted the contents. There were only two things in it and neither of them made my heart jump. One was a garage job-card with grease smears on it. At the top was printed, "Nelson's Garage, Salamanca, New York," and judging from the list of repairs required the car must have had an argument with a mountain. It was dated 4–11–40. The other item was sheets of printed matter. I unfolded them. They had been torn from the *Garden Journal*, which I would have recognized from the page and type without the running head, and the matter was an article entitled "Kurume Yellows in America" by Lewis Hewitt. I lifted the brows and handed it to Wolfe. Then my eye caught something I had missed on the garage job-card, something written in pencil on the reverse side. It was a name, "Pete Arango," and it was written in a small fine hand quite different from the scribbling on the face of the card. There was another sample of a similar small fine hand there in front of me, on the envelope at the top of the bundle addressed to Rose Lasher, and I untied the string and got out the letter and found that it was signed "Harry."

I passed the outfit to Wolfe and he looked it over.

He grunted. "This will interest the police." His eyes went to Rose. "Even more than your—"

"No!" she cried. She was wriggling. "You won't . . . oh, for God's sake, you mustn't—"

"Where did you hide in that corridor?"

She unloaded. She had hid in the corridor, yes, from the time I saw her there until some time after she had opened the door of the exhibit to look in. She had hid behind the packing cases and shrubs against the rear wall of the corridor. The sound of commotion had alarmed her, and she had sneaked out and gone to the main room and pushed into the crowd around the exhibit and I had returned her bag to her, which she had dropped without knowing it.

What and whom had she seen while hiding in the corridor?

Nothing. Maybe a few people, she didn't know who, passing by. Nothing and no one she remembered, except Fred Updegraff.

Of course she was lying. She must have seen Wolfe and Hewitt and me go by and me pick up the stick. The stick was there at the door that she was watching. And she must have seen someone leave the stick there, stoop down to pass the crook through the loop of the string, probably open the door to get hold of the loop which was ready inside, hidden among the foliage. But Wolfe was handicapped. He didn't dare mention the stick. That was out. But boy, did he want her to mention it, and incidentally mention who had walked in there with it and left it there?

Didn't he? He did. But she wouldn't. She was stuck

tight again, and I never saw Wolfe try harder and get nowhere. Finally he pulled the bluff of phoning Cramer, and even that didn't budge her. Then he gave up and rang for Fritz to bring beer.

At that point the phone rang and I answered it, and heard a familiar voice:

"Archie? Saul Panzer. May I speak to Mr. Wolfe?"

Wolfe took it on his phone, and I learned that during my absence he had got hold of Saul and sent him to the Flower Show. After getting a report he told Saul to drop the line he was on and come to the office. He hung up and leaned back and heaved a sigh, and regarded Rose with no sign of esteem.

"That," he said, "was a man I sent to collect facts about Mr. Gould. I'd rather get them from you. I'll allow you until tomorrow to jog your memory about what you saw in that corridor this afternoon, but you'll tell me about him now. We've got all night. How long had you known him?"

"About two years," she said sullenly.

"Are you his wife? His widow?"

She flushed and her lips tightened. "No. He said he wasn't the marrying kind. That's what he said."

"But he lived on Morrow Street with you?"

"No, he didn't. He only came there. He had a room in one of the houses on the Dill place on Long Island. No one ever knew about Morrow Street—I mean no one out there." She suddenly perked forward and her eyes flashed, and I was surprised at her spunk. "And no one's going to know about it! You hear that? Not while I'm alive they're not!"

"Do you have relatives on Long Island? Do your folks live there?"

"None of your business!"

"Perhaps not," Wolfe conceded. "I wouldn't want it to be. When and where did you meet Mr. Gould?"

She shut her mouth.

"Come," Wolfe said sharply. "Don't irritate me beyond reason. The next time I tell Mr. Goodwin to get Mr. Cramer on the phone it won't be a bluff."

She swallowed. "I was clerking in a store at Richdale and he—I met him there. That was nearly two years ago, when he was working at Hewitt's."

"Do you mean Lewis Hewitt's."

"Yes, the Hewitt estate."

"Indeed. What did he do there?"

"He was a gardener and he did some chauffeuring. Then he got fired. He always said he quit, but he got fired."

"When was that?"

"Over a year ago. Winter before last, it was. He was a good greenhouse man, and it wasn't long before he got another job at Dill's. That's about two miles the other side of Richdale. He went to live there in one of the houses."

"Did you live there with him?"

"Me?" She looked shocked and indignant. "I certainly didn't! I was living at home!"

"I beg your pardon. How long have you been living at the place on Morrow Street?"

She shut her mouth.

"Come, Miss Lasher. Even the janitor could tell me that."

"Look here," she said. "Harry Gould was no good. He never was any good. I knew that all the time. But the trouble is you get started, that's what makes the trouble, you get started and then you keep it up—even if I knew he was no good there was something about him. He always said he wasn't the marrying kind, but when he took me to that place on Morrow Street one day—that was last June, June last year—and said he had rented it, that looked like he wanted a home and maybe to get married after a while, so I quit my job and went there to live. That's how long

I've been living there, nine months. At first I was scared, and then I wasn't. There wasn't much money, but there was enough, and then I got scared again on account of the money. I didn't know where he got it."

The seam had ripped and the beans were tumbling out, and Wolfe sat back and let them come.

"He came there one night—he came four or five nights a week—that was one night in December not long before Christmas—and he had over a thousand dollars. He wouldn't let me count it, but it must have been, it might have been two or three thousand. He bought me a watch, and that was all right, but all the money did to me, it scared me. And he began to act different and he didn't come so often. And then about a month ago he told me he was going to get married."

Her lips went tight and after a moment she swallowed.

"Not to you," Wolfe said.

"Oh, no." She made a noise. "Me? Not so you could notice it. But he wouldn't tell me her name. And he kept having money. He didn't show it to me any more, but several times at night I looked in his pockets and he had a bankbook with over three thousand dollars in it and he always had a big roll of bills. Then yesterday I saw a picture of him in the paper, at the Flower Show with that girl. He hadn't said a word to me about it, not a word. And he hadn't been to Morrow Street for nearly a week, and he didn't come last night, so I went there today to see, and there he was in there with her. When I saw him in there with her I wanted to kill him, I tell you that straight, I wanted to kill him!"

"But you didn't," Wolfe murmured.

Her face worked. "I wanted to!"

"But you didn't."

"No," she said, "I didn't."

"But someone did." Wolfe's voice was silky. "He was

murdered. And naturally you are in sympathy with the effort to find the murderer. Naturally you intend to help—"

"I do not!"

"But my dear Miss Lasher—"

"I'm not your dear Miss Lasher." She leaned to him from the edge of the chair. "I know what I am, I'm a bum, that's what I am and I know it. But I'm not a complete dumbbell, see? Harry's dead, ain't he? Who killed him I don't know, maybe you did, or maybe it was that ten-cent Clark Gable there that thinks he's so slick he can slide uphill. Whoever it was, I don't know and I don't care, all I care about now is one thing, my folks aren't going to know anything about all this, none of it, and if it gets so I can't help it and they find out about it, all they'll have left to do with me is bury me."

She straightened up. "It's my honor," she said. "It's my family's honor."

Whether that came from the movies or wherever it came from, that's exactly what she said. I suspected the movies, considering her cheap crack about me being a ten-cent Clark Gable, which was ridiculous. He simpers, to begin with, and to end with no one can say I resemble a movie actor, and if they did it would be more apt to be Gary Cooper than Clark Gable.

Anyhow, that's what she said. And apparently she meant it, for although Wolfe went on patiently working at her he didn't get much. She didn't know why Harry had been fired from Hewitt's, or where his sudden wealth had come from, or why he had carefully saved that garage job-card, or why he had been interested in the Kurume yellows, which she had never heard of, and above all she couldn't remember anyone or anything she had seen while she was hiding in the corridor. Wolfe kept at her, and it looked as if she was in for a long hard night.

Around eleven o'clock an interruption arrived in the shape of Saul Panzer. I let him in and he went to the office. With one glance of his sharp gray eyes he added Rose to his internal picture gallery, which meant that she was there for good, and then stood there in his old brown suit—he never wore an overcoat—with his old brown cap in his hand. He looked like a relief veteran, whereas he owned two houses in Brooklyn and was the best head *and* foot detective west of the Atlantic.

"Miss Rose Lasher, Mr. Saul Panzer," Wolfe said. "Archie, get me the atlas."

I shrugged. One of his favorite ways of spending an evening was with the atlas, but with company there? Muttering, "Mine not to reason why," I took it to him, and sat down again while he went on his trip. Pretty soon he closed it and shoved it aside, and addressed Rose:

"Was Mr. Gould ever in Salamanca, New York?"

She said she didn't know.

"Those letters, Archie," Wolfe said.

I got the pile and gave him half and kept half for myself and ran through the envelopes. I was nearly at the bottom when Wolfe emitted a grunt of satisfaction.

"Here's a postcard he sent you from Salamanca on December 14th, 1940. A picture of the public library. It says, 'Will be back tomorrow or next day. Love and kisses. Harry.'"

"Then I guess he was there," Rose admitted sullenly.

"Archie, give Saul a hundred dollars." Wolfe handed Saul the postcard and the garage job-card. "Go to Salamanca. Take a plane to Buffalo and hire a car. Do you know what Harry Gould looked like?"

"Yes, sir."

"Note the dates—but I don't need to tell you. Go up there and get all you can. Phone me on arrival."

"Yes, sir. If necessary do I pay for it?"

Wolfe grimaced. "Within reason. I want all I can get. Make it two hundred, Archie."

I counted ten twenties into Saul's hand from the stack I got from the safe, and he stuffed it into his pocket and went, as usual, without any foolish questions.

Wolfe resumed with Rose, after ringing for beer. First he spent five minutes trying to get her to remember what Harry had gone to Salamanca for, or anything he had said to her about it, but that was a blank. No savvy Salamanca. Then he returned to former topics, but with a series of flanking movements. He discussed cooking with her. He asked about Harry's abilities and experience as a gardener, his pay, his opinion of Hewitt and Dill, his employers, his drinking habits and other habits.

I was busy getting it down in my notebook, but I certainly wasn't trembling with excitement. I knew that by that method, by the time dawn came Wolfe could accumulate a lot of facts that she wouldn't know he was getting, and one or two of them might even mean something, but among them would not be the thing we wanted most to know, what and who she had seen in the corridor. As it stood now we didn't dare to let the cops get hold of her even if we felt like it, for fear Cramer would open her up by methods of his own, and if he learned about the stick episode his brain might leap a barricade and spoil everything. And personally I didn't want to toss her to the lions anyhow, even after that Clark Gable crack.

It was a little after midnight when the doorbell rang again, and I went to answer it and got an unpleasant surprise. There on the stoop was Johnny Keems. I never resented any of the other boys being called in to work on a case, and I didn't actually resent Johnny either, only he gave me a pain in the back of my lap with his smirking around trying to edge in on my job. So I didn't howl with delight at sight of him, and then I nearly did howl, not with delight, when I saw he wasn't alone and what it was that kept him from being alone.

It was Anne Tracy standing behind him. And standing behind her was Fred Updegraff.

"Greetings," I said, concealing my emotions, and they all entered. And the sap said to her, "This way, Miss Tracy," and started for the office with her!

I stepped around and blocked him. "Some day," I said, "you'll skin your nose. Wait in the front room."

He smiled at me the way he does. I waited until all three of them had gone through the door to the front room and it had closed behind them, and then returned to the office and told Wolfe:

"I didn't know you had called out the army while I was gone. Visitors. The guy who wants my job and is welcome to it at any time, and my future wife, and the wholesome young fellow with the serious chin."

"Ah," Wolfe said. "That's like Johnny. He should have phoned." He grunted. He leaned back. His eyes rested on Rose an instant, then they closed, and his lips pushed out, and in, and out and in.

His eyes opened. "Bring them in here."

"But—" Rose began, starting from her chair.

"It's all right," he assured her.

I wasn't so darned sure it was all right, but it was him that wanted the black orchids, not me, so I obeyed orders, went to the front room by the connecting doors, and told them to come in. Johnny, who is a gentleman from his skin out, let Anne and Fred pass through ahead of him. She stopped in the middle of the room.

"How do you do," Wolfe said politely. "Forgive me for not rising; I rarely do. May I introduce—Miss Rose Lasher, Miss Anne Tracy. By the way, Miss Lasher has just been telling me that you were engaged to marry Mr. Gould."

"That's a lie," Anne said.

She looked terrible. At no time during the afternoon, when the turmoil had started or when Cramer had announced it was murder or when he had marched her out for examination, had she shown any sign of sag or yellow, but now she looked as if she had taken all she could. At least she did when she entered, and maybe that is why she reacted the way she did to Wolfe's statement and got rough.

"Marry Harry Gould?" she said. "That isn't true!" Her voice trembled with something that sounded like scorn but might have been anything.

Rose was out of her chair and was trembling all over. All right, I thought, Wolfe arranged for it and now he'll get it. She'll scratch Anne's eyes out. I moved a step. But she didn't. She even tried to control her voice.

"You bet it ain't true!" she cried, and that *was* scorn. "Harry wasn't marrying into *your* family! He wasn't marrying any daughter of a thief!"

Anne gawked at her.

Rose spat. "You with your stuckup nose! Why ain't your father in jail where he belongs? And you up there showing your legs like a ten-cent floozie—"

"Archie," Wolfe said sharply. "Take her upstairs."

Rose went on, not even hearing him. I got her suitcase in one hand and gripped her arm with the other and turned her around, and the idea of her nonmarrying Harry marrying another girl, in spite of his being dead, occupied her brain so that she kept right on spitting compliments without even knowing I was propelling her out of the room until we were in the hall. Then she went flat-footed and shut her mouth and glared at me.

"On up two flights," I said. "Or I know how to carry you so you can't bite." I still had her arm. "Up we go, sister."

She came. I took her into the spare room on the same

floor as mine, switched on the lights, and put her suitcase on a chair.

I pointed. "Ten-cent bathroom there. Ten-cent bed there. You won't be needed—"

She sat down on the bed and started to bawl.

I went down to the kitchen and told Fritz, "Lady guest in the south room. She has her own nightie, but would you mind seeing about towels and flowers in her room? I'm busy."

Chapter 7

Anne slept in my bed that night.

It went like this. When I got back to the office Anne was in my chair with her elbows on the desk and her hands covering her eyes. That was a favorite trick of Johnny's, putting someone else in my chair. He hadn't tried putting himself in it again since the day a couple of years back when I found him there looking at my notebook and sort of lost my temper.

Fred Updegraff was on a chair against the wall and Johnny was standing in front of Wolfe's desk. Evidently Wolfe had made some pointed remarks, for Johnny didn't look at all cocky.

"Yes, sir," he was saying in a hurt tone, "but the Tracys live in humble circumstances and have no phone, so I used my best judgment—"

"You were at the Tracy home? Where is it?"

"In Richdale, Long Island, sir. My instructions were to investigate Anne Tracy. I learned that she lives in Richdale, where the Dill nurseries and offices are. You know she works there—"

"I was aware of that. Be brief."

"Yes, sir. I went out to Richdale and made inquiries. I

contacted a young woman—as you know, I am especially effective with young women--"

"Contact is not a verb and I said be brief."

"Yes, sir. The last time you told me that I looked it up in the dictionary and I certainly don't want to contradict you but it says contact is a verb. Transitive or intransitive."

"Contact is not a verb under this roof."

"Yes, sir. I learned that Miss Tracy's father had worked at Dill's for many years, up to about a year ago. He was assistant superintendent in charge of broad-leaved evergreens. Dill discovered he was kiting shipments and fired him."

"Kiting shipments?"

"Yes, sir. On shipments to a big estate in Jersey, the Cullen place. He would ship two hundred rhododendrons instead of one hundred and collect from Cullen for the extra hundred personally, at half price. It amounted to several thousand dollars."

Anne lifted her head and turned it and made a noise of protest.

"Miss Tracy says it was only sixteen hundred dollars," Johnny said. "I'm telling you what I was told. People exaggerate, and this never was made public, and Tracy wasn't arrested. He stole it to pay a specialist for fixing his son's eyes, something wrong with his son's eyes. He can't get another job. His daughter was Dill's secretary and still is. She gets fifty a week and pays back twenty on what her father stole, so I was told. She refuses to verify those figures."

Wolfe looked at Anne.

"It doesn't matter," Anne said, looking at me. "Does it?"

"I suppose not," Wolfe said, but if it's wrong, correct it."

"It's wrong. I get twenty dollars a week and I pay back ten."

"Good God," I blurted, "you need a union."

That was probably Freudian. Probably subconsciously I meant she needed a union with me. So I added hastily, "I mean a labor union. Twenty bucks a week!"

Johnny looked annoyed. He's a conservative. "So of course that gave me an in. I went to Miss Tracy's home and explained to her confidentially the hole she was in. That this murder investigation would put the police on to her father's crime, and that she and Dill were compounding a felony, which is against the law, and that the police would have to be fixed or they'd all be in jail, and there was only one man I knew of who could fix it because he was on intimate terms with high police officials, and that was Mr. Nero Wolfe. I said she'd better come and see you immediately, and she came. It was nearly eleven o'clock and there was no train in from Richdale, so we took a taxi."

Johnny shot me a glance, as much as to say, "Try and match that one."

"How far is it to Richdale?" Wolfe demanded.

"From here? Oh, twenty-five miles."

"How much was the taxi fare?"

"Eight dollars and forty cents counting the tip. The bridge—"

"Don't put it on expense. Pay it yourself."

"But—but, sir—Archie always brings people here—"

"Pay it yourself. You are not Archie. Thank God. One Archie is enough. I sent you to get facts, not Miss Tracy—certainly I didn't send you to coerce her with preposterous threats and fables about my relations with the police. Go to the kitchen—no. Go home."

"But, sir—"

"Go home. And for God's sake quit trying to imitate Archie. You'll never make it. Go home."

Johnny went.

Wolfe asked the guests if they would like some beer and they shook their heads. He poured a glass for himself, drank some, wiped his lips, and leaned back.

"Then—" Anne began, but it got caught on the way out. She cleared her throat and swallowed, and tried again. "Then what he said—you said his threat was preposterous. You mean the police won't do that—won't arrest my father?"

"I couldn't say, Miss Tracy. The police are unpredictable. Even so, that is highly improbable." Wolfe's eyes left her. "And you, Mr. Updegraff? By what bold stroke did Mr. Keems bring you along?"

"He didn't bring me." Fred stood up. "I came."

"By pure coincidence? Or automatism?"

Fred moved forward and put a hand on the back of my chair, which Anne was still sitting in. "I'm protecting Miss Tracy."

"Oh. From what?"

"From everything," he said firmly. He appeared to have a tendency to talk too loud, and he looked more serious than ever, and the more serious he looked the younger he looked. At that moment he might even have passed for Anne's younger brother, which was okay, since I had no objection if she wanted to be a sister to him.

"That's quite a job," Wolfe said. "Are you a friend of hers?"

"I'm more than a friend!" Fred declared defiantly. Suddenly he got as red as a peony. "I mean I—she let me take her home."

"You were there when Mr. Keems arrived?"

"Yes. We had just got there. And I insisted on coming along. It sounded to me like a frame-up. I thought he was lying; I didn't think he was working for you. It didn't sound—I've heard my father talk about you. He met you once—you probably don't remember—"

Wolfe nodded. "At the Atlantic States Exposition. How is he?"

"Oh, he's—not very good." Fred's color was normal again. "He gave up when we lost the plantation of rhodaleas—he just sat down and quit. He had spent his whole life on it, and of course it was an awful wallop financially too. I suppose you know about it."

"I read of it, yes. The Kurume yellows." Wolfe was sympathetic but casual. "And by the way, someone told me, I forget who, that your father was convinced that his plantation was deliberately infected by Lewis Hewitt, out of pique—or was it Watson or Dill he suspected?"

"He suspected all of them." Fred looked uncomfortable. "Everybody. But that was just—he was hardly responsible, it broke him up so. He had been holding back over thirty varieties, the best ones, for ten years, and was going to start distribution this spring. It was simply too much for Dad to take."

Wolfe grunted. "It seems to be still on your mind too. Mr. Goodwin tells me you invaded Rucker and Dill's exhibit this afternoon and made off with an infected twig. As a souvenir?"

"I—" Fred hesitated. "I guess that was dumb. Of course it's still on my mind—it darned near ruined us. I wanted to test that twig and see if it was Kurume yellows that had somehow got into the exhibits."

"And investigate the how?"

"I might have. I might have tried to."

"You never traced the infection of your plantation?"

"No. We hadn't had a thing for two years from any of the people that had had Kurume yellows, except a few Ilex crenata as a gift from Hewitt, and they were from nowhere near his infected area and we had them half a mile from the rhodaleas." Fred gestured impatiently. "But that's old prunings. What I was saying, I didn't think you'd pull a trick like that on Miss Tracy." A look came into his eyes. "Now I can take her back home."

The look in his eye took me back to high school days. It was the hand-holding look. Flutter, my heart, bliss looms and ecstasy, I shall hold her little hand in mine! I looked at Anne with pride. A girl who could enkindle Lewis Hewitt to the extent of a black orchid and a dinner on Tuesday, and on Thursday forment the hand-holding hankering in a pure young peony-grower—a girl with a reach like that was something.

At that moment, I admit, she wasn't so overwhelming. She looked pretty dilapidated. She said to Wolfe, "I have to be at the District Attorney's office at ten in the morning. I said I would. I don't mind them asking me questions about that—what happened there today—but what I'm afraid of now, I'm afraid they'll ask me about my father. If they do, what am I going to say? Am I going to admit—" She stopped and her lip started to tremble and she put her teeth on it.

"You need a lawyer," Fred declared. "I'll get one. I don't know any in New York—"

"I do," Wolfe said. "Sit down, Mr. Updegraff." His eyes moved to Anne. "There's a bed here, Miss Tracy, and you'd better use it. You look tired. I doubt if the police will ask you about your father. If they do, don't answer. Refer them to Mr. Dill. They're much more apt to be inquisitive about your engagement to marry Mr. Gould."

"But I wasn't!"

"Apparently he thought you were."

"But he couldn't. He knew very well I didn't like him! And he—" She stopped.

"He what?"

"I won't say that. He's dead."

"Had he asked you to marry him?"

"Yes, he had."

"And you refused?"

"Yes."

"But you consented to perform that rustic charade at the Flower Show with him?"

"I didn't know he was going to be in it—not when Mr. Dill asked me to do it, about two months ago, when he first thought of it. It was going to be another man, a young man in the office. Then Mr. Dill told me Harry Gould was going to do it. I didn't like him, but I didn't want to object because I couldn't afford to offend—I mean Mr. Dill had been so kind about my father—not having him arrested and letting me pay it off gradually—"

"Call it kind if you want to," Fred blurted indignantly. "My lord, your father had worked for him for twenty years!"

Wolfe ignored him. "Was Mr. Gould pestering you? About marrying him?"

"Not pestering me, no. I was—" Anne bit her lip. "I just didn't like him."

"Had you known him long?"

"Not very long. I'm in the office and he was outside. I met him, I don't know, maybe three months ago."

"Did your father know him?"

She shook her head. "I don't think they ever met. Father was—had left before Harry came to work there. Harry used to work on the Hewitt estate on the other side of Richdale."

"So I understand. Do you know why he quit?"

"No, I didn't know him then."

"Have you any idea who killed him?"

"No," she said.

I lifted a brow, not ostentatiously. She said it too quick and she shaded it wrong. There was enough change in tempo and tone to make it at least ten to one that she was telling a whopper. That was bad. Up to that everything had been wholesome and straightforward, and all of a sudden without any warning that big fly plopped in the milk. I cocked an eye at Fred, and of course he hadn't caught it. But Wolfe had. His eyes had gone nearly shut.

He started after her. He kept it polite and friendly, but he went at her from every angle and direction. And for the second time that night he got the can sent back empty by a juvenile female. After a solid hour of it he didn't have even a hint of what it was she was keeping tucked away under her hair, whether it was a suspicion or a fact or a deduction she had made from a set of circumstances. Neither did I. But she was sitting on some kind of lid, and she was smart enough to see that Wolfe knew it and was trying to jostle her off.

It was half past one when Fred Updegraff looked at his watch and stood up again and said it was late and he would take Miss Tracy home.

Wolfe shook his head. "She's exhausted and it's twenty-five miles and there are no trains. She can sleep here. I want to speak to her in the morning before she goes to the District Attorney's office. Archie, will you please see that the north room is in order?"

That meant my room and my bed. Anne started to protest, but not with much spirit, and I went and got Fritz and took him upstairs with me to help change sheets and towels. As I selected a pajama suit for her from the drawer, tan with brown stripes, and put it on the turned down sheet, I reflected that things were moving pretty fast, considering that it was less than ten hours since she had first spoken to me and we never had actually been introduced. Fritz took my sheets and pillow and a blanket downstairs and I went up one flight to the plant rooms and cut three black orchids, one from each plant, and returned and put them in a vase on the bed table. Hewitt had given her one.

On my way downstairs I stopped at the door to the south room and listened. No sound. I tried the door; it was bolted on the inside. I knocked, not very loud. Rose's voice came:

"Who is it?"

"Clark Gable," I called. "Good night, Ruby."

In the lower hall I met Anne coming out of the office, escorted by Fritz. I suppose it would have been more genteel to take her up myself, but it would have been a temptation to get sentimental there among my own furniture, so I told her good night and let her go. In the office Wolfe was alone, in his chair with his arms folded and his chin down; evidently Fred had departed. I began taking cushions from the couch and tossing them into a corner, getting ready to fix my bed.

"Two of them," Wolfe growled.

"Two of what?"

"Women. Nannygoats."

"Not Anne. She's more like a doe. More like a gazelle."

"Bah."

"More like a swan." I flipped a sheet over the couch and tucked it in. "I put three black orchids at her bedside. One from each plant."

"I told Theodore to put them in the fumigating room."

"He did. That's where I found them." I spread the blanket. "I thought we might as well get all the pleasure we can put out of them before they're returned to Hewitt."

"They're not going to be returned."

"Oh, I expect they are." I hung my coat and vest over a chair and sat down to take off my shoes. "It seems a pity.

Two girls up there in bed, and if you knew what they know, or probably what either one of them knows, you'd have it sewed up. Rose actually saw the murderer set the trap. I don't know what Anne saw or heard, but she sure does. It's a darned shame. With all your finesse . . ." I got my pants off. ". . . all your extraordinary gifts . . ." I removed my shirt. ". . . all your acknowledged genius, your supreme talent in the art of inquest . . ."

He got up and stalked from the room without a word. I called a cheery good night after him but heard no reply, and after performing a few bedtime chores such as bolting the front door, I laid me down to sleep.

I overdid it. With the house full of company, I intended to be up and about bright and early, but when something jangled my brain alive and I realized it was the phone ringing, I opened my eyes and glanced at my wrist and saw it was after eight o'clock. It was Saul Panzer on the phone calling from Salamanca. I put him through to Wolfe's room and was told by Wolfe that no record would be required, which was his polite way of telling me to hang up, so I did. A trip to Fritz in the kitchen got me the information that Wolfe already had his breakfast tray, and so did Anne and Rose. I washed and dressed in a hurry, returned to the kitchen for my morning refreshment of grapefruit, ham and eggs, muffins and coffee, and was finishing my second cup when the doorbell rang. Fritz was upstairs at the moment, so I went for it, and through the glass panel saw it was Inspector Cramer, unattended.

The situation had aspects. Rose might come trotting downstairs any minute, and if she chose the minute that Cramer was in the hall, that would be the last we would see of Rose. But any delay in opening up would make Cramer suspicious. I swung the door open.

"Law and order forever," I said cordially. "Come in."

"Nuts," he said, entering.

So for that incivility I let him hang up his hat and coat himself. By the time he had done that I had the door closed and was on the other side of him. He screwed up his face at me and demanded:

"Where is she?"

Chapter 8

I grinned to the best of my ability. "Now wait a minute," I said in a grieved tone. "I've been up less than an hour and my brain's not warmed up. In the first place, how could I know she was married? In the second—"

He made a noise and moved. I moved, sort of backward. The maneuver ended with me covering the foot of the stairs, which was across the hall from the door to the office, and him pressing forward without actually touching me. There I stopped and he had to.

"I'm going up to see Wolfe," he said as if he meant it. "I am aware that he spends the morning with his goddamn posies and refuses to come down before eleven o'clock. So I'm going up. Stand aside."

He moved again and we made contact (noun), but I merely held it. "This," I said, "is pretty damn silly. I didn't have to let you in and you know it, but I did. What do you think this is, the den of the White Slave King? This is Nero Wolfe's home, and there's his office where he receives callers, and for last year his income tax was eleven thousand four hundred and twelve dollars and eighty-three cents and he paid it last week. Do you remember what happened the time Purley took me down and charged me with interfering with an officer in the performance of his duty? Wasn't that a picnic?"

He swung on his heel and tramped into the office. I followed, and shut the door, and stayed between him and it until he had sat down. Then, knowing I could move at least twice as fast as he could, I went to my desk.

"Now," I inquired pleasantly, "where is who?"

He regarded me with a mean eye. "Last night," he said, "one of Wolfe's men took Anne Tracy from her home in Richdale. My man covering the house recognized him and phoned in. I had a man out front when they arrived here. Your man soon left, and so did the Updegraff boy, later, but she hasn't left up to now. Where is she?"

So our little Rose was still safe. I locked my relief in my breast and looked crestfallen.

"I guess it's your trick, Inspector," I admitted. "Miss Tracy is upstairs in my bed. She spent the night there."

He got red. He's a terrible prude. "See here, Goodwin—"

"No no no no," I said hastily. "Rinse your mind out. I slept here on the couch. And I doubt if she's in my bed at that, because she's probably up and dressed. She has a date at the D.A.'s office at ten o'clock, and it's nine thirty now."

"Then you admit she's here."

"Admit it? I'm proud of it."

"Where is she, up with Wolfe?"

"I don't know. I got up late. I just finished breakfast."

"Find out. Tell her the appointment at the D.A.'s office is off. I want to see her as soon as I finish with you."

I plugged in the plant room extension and gave it a buzz. In a minute Wolfe's voice was in my ear:

"Archie? It's about time. Get Mr. Hewitt—"

"Hold it," I put in. "Reporting bad luck. Inspector Cramer is sitting here glaring at me. Johnny was spotted last night, and Miss Tracy is not to go to the D.A.'s office because Cramer wants to see her as soon as he gets through with me. He seems to be disgruntled about something."

"Does he know who slept in the south room?"

"I think not. I'm sure not."

"Very well. I'll attend to that. Miss Tracy is here with me. She can go down whenever. Mr. Cramer is ready for her. Get Mr. Hewitt on the phone."

"Right out loud?"

"Certainly."

I disconnected and told Cramer, "Miss Tracy is up helping with the orchids and will be available when wanted. Excuse me." I found Hewitt's Long Island number and requested it, and finally got him via two butlers and a secretary, and put him through to Wolfe. Then I swiveled around and crossed my legs and clasped my hands back of my head.

"Okay, Inspector. I'm disengaged for the moment. What shall we talk about?"

"Murder."

"Fine. Any particular murder?"

Cramer took a cigar from his pocket and put it in his mouth and took it out again. He was controlling himself. "I hand it to you," he said. "For barefaced lying I'd play you on the nose. Up there yesterday. You didn't know anyone or anything. But—" He put the cigar back in his mouth. "But you've been hanging around there all week. Every day. And then a man gets murdered and there you are. You *and* Nero Wolfe."

I nodded sympathetically. "I admit it looks sinister. But as I told you yesterday, Wolfe sent me there to look at orchids."

"There were no orchids in the Rucker and Dill exhibit."

"No, but there was—you know what there was. You've seen her. And I'm only a man after all—"

"All right, clown it. Yesterday afternoon about twenty minutes past four you were seen by young Updegraff, with Wolfe and Lewis Hewitt, in the corridor back of the Rucker and Dill exhibit. What were you doing there?"

"Well." I hesitated. "If I told you I was pulling the string that fired the shot that killed Harry Gould, would you believe me?"

"No."

"Then I won't. We were walking from one place to another place."

"You didn't mention yesterday that you were in that corridor at that time."

"Excuse it. Oversight."

"Maybe. What were you saying to Ruby Lawson yesterday?"

"Ruby—?" I frowned. "Oh. Her. You mean after I told Purley she was a Chinese spy. I was trying to date her up. You see, looking at Miss Tracy so much had aroused—"

"I'll bet it had. Did you date her?"

"Yes."

"When is it?"

"Not is it, was it. She didn't keep it."

"That's too bad. What was in the note Miss Tracy's father gave you to take to her?"

"Now, Inspector," I said reprovingly. "I didn't write the note and it wasn't addressed to me."

"Had you met her father before?"

"Never. Didn't know him from Adam."

"Wasn't it peculiar that he entrusted a perfect stranger with an important message to his daughter at a time like that?"

"Not very. He saw me entering the office. People trust me on sight. It's my face, especially my eyes."

"I see. That talk Wolfe had to have with Lewis Hewitt.

So important he had to have it then and there, murder or no murder."

Cramer chewed his cigar.

"Yes, sir," I said.

"So important he had to have you to take notes of it."

"Yes, sir."

"I'd like to see the notes you took."

I shook my head regretfully. "Sorry, confidential business. Ask Wolfe."

"I intend to. You won't show me the notes?"

"Certainly not."

"Very well. Now. Last but not least. Why did Wolfe send a man out to Richdale last night to get Anne Tracy?"

"Search me. I wasn't here when he sent him."

"Were you here when she came?"

"Yes."

"Well?"

I grinned at him. "When I was a kid out in Ohio we had a swell comeback for that. If someone said 'Well?' to you, you said, 'Enough wells will make a river.' Wasn't that a stunner?"

"You bet it was. Had Lewis Hewitt engaged Wolfe to arrange for payment to W. G. Dill of the amount Anne Tracy's father had stolen, and get a release?"

I stared at him. "By golly, that's an idea," I said enthusiastically. "That's pretty cute. Hewitt took her to dinner—"

The door opened and Fritz entered. I nodded at him.

"A young man," Fritz said, being discreet.

"Who?" I asked. "Don't mind the Inspector; he already knows everything in the world—"

Fritz didn't get a chance to tell me, because the young man came bouncing in. It was Fred Updegraff. He stopped in the middle of the room, saw Cramer, said, "Oh," looked at me and demanded:

"Where's Miss Tracy?"

I surveyed him disapprovingly. "That's no way to behave," I told him. "Inspector Cramer is grilling me. Go to the front room and wait your turn—"

"No." Cramer stood up. "Get Miss Tracy down here and I'll take her to the front room. I want to see her before I have a talk with Wolfe, and then we can all go to the D.A.'s office together."

"The hell we can," I remarked.

"The hell we can. Send for her."

I sent Fritz. He used the elevator, since a lady was involved. In the office you could hear it creaking and groaning up, and pretty soon it came down again and jolted to a stop. When Anne entered Fred looked at her the way a blind man looks at the sun. I hoped I wasn't that obvious, and anyway she wasn't very sunny. She tried to greet us with a kind of smile, but with the red-rimmed eyes and the corners of the mouth down it certainly wasn't the face that had stolen the show from a million flowers.

Cramer took her to the front room and shut the soundproof door behind him. I went to my desk and took advantage of this first chance to open the morning mail. Fred wandered around restlessly, looking at the titles of books on the shelves, and finally sat down and lit a cigarette.

"Am I in the way?" he asked.

"Not at all," I assured him.

"Because if I am I can wait outdoors. Only I got a little chilly. I've been out there since eight o'clock."

I abandoned the mail to swivel around and stare at him in awe.

"Good God," I said, stupefied. "You win." I waved a hand. "You can have her."

"Have her?" He flushed. "What are you talking about? Who do you think you are?"

"Brother," I said, "who I am can be left to the worms

that eventually eat me, but I know who I am not. I am not a guy who swims the Hellespont, nor him who—he who flees the turmoil of battle to seek you know what on the silken cushions of Cleopatra's barge. I'm not the type—"

The phone rang and I put the receiver to my ear and heard Wolfe's voice: "Archie, come up here."

"Right away," I said, and arose and asked Fred, "Which do you want, whisky or hot coffee?"

"Coffee, if it's not—"

"Righto. Come with me."

I turned him over to Fritz in the kitchen and mounted the three flights to the plant rooms. It was a sunny day and some of the mats were drawn, but mostly the glass was clear, especially in the first two rooms, and the glare and blaze of color was dazzling. In the long stretch where the germinating flasks were, of course the glass was painted. Theodore Horstmann was there examining the flasks. I opened the door into the potting room, and after taking one step stopped and sniffed. My nose is good and I knew that odor. One glance at Wolfe there on his special stool, which is more like a throne, showed me that he was alive, so I dived across to the wall and grabbed the valve to turn it. It was shut tight.

"What's the matter?" Wolfe inquired peevishly.

"I smelled ciphogene. I still do."

"I know. Theodore fumigated those plants a little while ago and opened the door too soon. There's not enough to do any harm."

"Maybe not," I muttered, "but I wouldn't trust that stuff on top of the Empire State Building on a windy day." The door to the fumigating room was standing open and I glanced inside. The benches were empty, as well as I could tell in the half dark. It had no glass. The smell didn't seem any stronger inside. I returned to Wolfe.

"How's Mr. Cramer?" he asked. "Stewing?"

I looked at him suspiciously. His asking that, and the tone of his voice, and the expression on his face—any one would have been enough for me the way I knew him, and the three together made it so obvious that the only question was how he got that way.

I confronted him. "Which one did you crack?" I demanded. "Rose or Anne?"

"Neither," he replied complacently. "I had an hour's talk with Miss Lasher while you were still sleeping, and later some conversation with Miss Tracy. They still clutch their secrets. When Mr. Hewitt—"

"Then where did you lap up all the cream? What are you gloating about?"

"I'm not gloating." He cocked his massive head on one side and rubbed his nose with a forefinger. "It is true that I have conceived a little experiment."

"Oh, you have. Goody. Before or after Cramer carts us off to the D.A.'s office?"

Wolfe chuckled. "Is that his intention? Then it must be before. Is Miss Tracy with him?"

"Yes. The youthful Updegraff is in the kitchen. He's going to marry Anne provided your experiment doesn't land him in the coop for murder."

"I thought you were affianced to Miss Tracy."

"That's off. If I married her he'd stand around in front of the house and make me nervous. He's started it already."

"Well, that saves us the trouble of sending for him. Keep him. When Mr. Hewitt arrives send him up to me immediately. Go down and get Mr. Dill on the phone and put him through to me. On your way make sure that Miss Lasher is in her room and going to stay there and not have hysterics. Except for Mr. Dill, and Mr. Hewitt when he comes, don't disturb me. I have some details to work out. And by the way, do not mention ciphogene."

His tone and look of smug self-satisfaction were absolutely insufferable. Not only that, as I well knew, they were a sign of danger for everyone concerned. When he was in that mood God alone could tell what was going to happen.

I went back through the plant rooms to the door to the stairs with my fingers crossed.

Chapter 9

It was nearly an hour later, 11:45, and I was alone in the office, when the door to the front room opened and Anne and Cramer entered. She looked mad and determined, and Cramer didn't appear to be exactly exultant, so I gathered that no great friendship had burst its bud.

"Where's Updegraff?" Cramer asked.

"Upstairs."

"I want to see Wolfe."

I buzzed the house phone, got an answer, held a brief conversation, and told the Inspector:

"He says to come up. Hewitt and Dill are up there."

"I'd rather see him down here."

That irritated me, and anyway I was already jumpy, waiting for Wolfe's experiment to start exploding. "My God," I said, "you're fussy. On arrival you insist on going upstairs right through me or over me. Now you have to be coaxed. If you want him down here go up and get him."

He turned. "Come, Miss Tracy, please."

She hesitated. I said, "Fred's up there. Let's all go."

I led the way and they followed. I took the elevator because the stairway route went within ten feet of the door to the south room and Rose might pick that moment to sneeze.

I was half expecting to see one of the peony-growers tied up and the other three applying matches to his bare feet, but not at all. We single-filed through twenty thousand orchids in the four plant rooms and entered the potting room, and there they were in the fumigating room, with the lights turned on, chatting away like pals. In the potting room Theodore was sloshing around with a hose, washing old pots.

"Good morning, Mr. Cramer!" Wolfe called. "Come in!"

Theodore was so enthusiastic with the hose that spray was flying around, and we all stepped into the fumigating room. Fred and Dill were there, seated on the lower tier of a staggered bench, and Wolfe was showing Hewitt a sealed joint in the wall. He was leaning on the handle of an osmundine fork, like a giant shepherd boy resting on his staff, and was expounding with childish enthusiasm:

". . . so we can stick them in here and close the door, and do the job with a turn of the valve I showed you in the potting room, and go on with our work outside. Twice a year at the most we do the whole place, and we use ciphogene for that, too. It's a tremendous improvement over the old methods. You ought to try it."

Hewitt nodded. "I think I will. I've been tempted to, but I was apprehensive about it, such deadly stuff."

Wolfe shrugged. "Anything you use is dangerous. You can't kill bugs and lice and eggs and spores with incense. And the cost of installation is a small item, unless you include a sealed chamber, which I would certainly advise—"

"Excuse *me*," Cramer said sarcastically.

Wolfe turned. "Oh, yes, you wanted to speak to me." He sidled around the end of a bench, sat down on a packing box, gradually giving it his weight, and kept himself upright with nothing to lean against, holding the osmundine fork perpendicular, with the handle-end resting on the floor, like Old King Cole with his scepter. He simpered at the Inspector, if an elephant can simper.

"Well, sir?"

Cramer shook his head. "I want you and Goodwin and Miss Tracy. So does the District Attorney. At his office."

"You don't mean that, Mr. Cramer."

"And why the hell—why don't I mean it?"

"Because you know I rarely leave my home. Because you know that citizens are not obligated to regulate their movements by the caprice of the District Attorney or to dart around frantically at your whim. We've had this out before. Have you an order from a court?"

"No."

"Then if you have questions to ask, ask them. Here I am."

"I can get an order from a court. And the D.A. is sore and probably will."

"We've had that out before, too. You know what you'll get if you try it." Wolfe shook his head regretfully. "Apparently you'll never learn. Confound you, you can't badger me. No one on earth can badger me except Mr. Goodwin. Why the devil do you rile me by trying it? It's a pity, because I'm inclined to help you. And I could help you. Do you want me to do you a favor?"

If the man who knew Wolfe best was me, next to me came Inspector Cramer. Over and over again through the years, he tried bluster because it was in his system and had to come out, but usually he knew when to drop it. So after narrowing his eyes at Wolfe without answering, he kicked a packing box a couple of feet to where there was more leg room, sat down and said calmly:

"Yeah, I'd love to have you do me a favor."

"Good, Archie, bring Miss Lasher up here."

I went. On my way downstairs I thought, so here she

goes to the wolves. I didn't like it. I wasn't especially fond of her, but my pride was hurt. It wasn't like Wolfe; it wasn't like us at all.

She was standing looking out of a window, biting her nails. The minute she saw me she started on a torrent. She couldn't stand it any longer, cooped up like that, she had to get out of there, she had to use a telephone—

"Okay," I said, "come up and say good-bye to Wolfe."

"But where am I going—what am I doing—"

"Discuss it with him."

I steered her up the one flight and through to the potting room. I had left the door to the fumigating room nearly closed so she couldn't see the assemblage until she was on the threshold, and as I opened it and ushered her in I took a better hold on her arm as a precaution in case she decided to go for Wolfe's eyes as souvenirs. But the reaction was the opposite of what I expected. She saw Cramer and went stiff. She stood stiff three seconds and then turned her head to me and said between her teeth:

"You lousy bastard."

They all stared at her.

Especially Cramer. Finally he spoke not to her but to Wolfe, "This is quite a favor. Where did you get her?"

"Sit down, Miss Lasher," Wolfe said.

"You might as well," I told her. "It's a party."

Her face white and her lips tight, she went and dropped onto a bench. The others were all sitting on benches or packing boxes.

"I told you this morning," Wolfe said, "that unless you told me what you saw in that corridor I would have to turn you over to the police."

She didn't say anything and didn't look as if she intended to.

"So, your name's Lasher," Cramer growled. "You might as well—"

"I think," Wolfe put in, "I can save you some time. Details can be supplied later. Her name is Rose Lasher. Yesterday at the Flower Show she saw Miss Tracy and Mr. Gould in Mr. Dill's exhibit. She wished to discuss an extremely important matter with Miss Tracy, so—"

"With me?" It popped out of Anne. She looked indignant. "There was nothing she could possibly—"

"Please, Miss Tracy." Wolfe was peremptory. "This will go better without interruptions. So, to intercept Miss Tracy on her exit, Miss Lasher found her way to the corridor and hid among the shrubs and packing cases along the rear wall opposite the door labeled 'Rucker and Dill.' That was at or about half past three. She remained concealed there until after half past four, and she was watching that door. Therefore she must have seen whatever went on there during that hour or more."

There were stirrings and sounds, then silence, except for the hissing of Theodore's hose in the potting room and the slapping and sloshing of the water against the pots. Wolfe told me to shut the door, and I did so, and then sat on the bench next to W. G. Dill.

"Okay," Cramer said dryly, "details later. What did she see?"

"She prefers not to say. Will you tell us now, Miss Lasher?"

Rose's eyes moved to him and away again, and that was all.

"Sooner or later you will," Wolfe declared. "Mr. Cramer will see to that. He can be—persuasive. In the meantime, I'll tell you what you saw, at least part of it. You saw a man approach that door with a cane in his hand. He was furtive, he kept an eye on the corridor in both directions, and he was in a hurry. You saw him open the door and close it again, and kneel or stoop, doing something with his hands, and when he went away he left the cane there on the floor, its crook against the crack at the bottom of the door. You saw that, didn't you?"

Rose didn't even look at him.

"Very well. I don't know what time that happened, except that it was between four and four-twenty. Probably around four o'clock. The next episode I do know. At twenty minutes past four you saw three men come along the corridor. They saw the cane and spoke about it. One of them picked it up, brushed a loop of green string from the crook, and handed it to one of the others. I don't know whether you saw the string or not. I'm certain that you didn't know that it was part of a longer string that had been tied to the trigger of a revolver, and that by picking up the cane the man had fired the revolver and killed Harry Gould. Nor did you know their names, though you do now. Mr. Goodwin picked up the cane and handed it to Mr. Hewitt. The man with them was myself."

Wolfe took something from his vest pocket, with his left hand, because his right was holding the osmundine fork for support. "Here's the piece of string that was looped on the cane. Not that I would expect you to identify it. I may as well say here that the cane was handed to Mr. Hewitt because it was his property."

He handed the string to Cramer.

I was sunk. Ordinarily, in such circumstances, I would have been watching faces and movements, and hearing what sounds were made or words blurted, but this time he had me. He looked as if he was in his right mind, with all the assured arrogance of Nero Wolfe salting away another one, but either he was cuckoo or I was. He was not only spilling the beans; he was smashing the dish. In any conceivable case it was good-bye orchids. I looked at Hewitt.

And Hewitt should have been half astonished and half sore, and he wasn't. He was pale, and he was trying to pretend he wasn't pale. He was staring at Wolfe, and he licked his lips—the end of his tongue came out and went in, and then came out again.

Uh-uh, I thought. So that's it. But my God, then—

Cramer was looking at the string. W. G. Dill asked, "May I see it?" and held out a hand, and Cramer gave it to him but kept his eyes on it.

"Of course," Wolfe said, "the point is, not who picked the cane up, but who put it there. Miss Lasher, who saw him do it, could tell us but prefers not to. She claims she didn't see him. So we'll have to get at it by indirection. Here are some facts that may help—but it isn't any too comfortable in here. Shall we move downstairs?"

"No," Hewitt said. "Go ahead and finish."

"Go ahead," Cramer said. He reached for the string and Dill handed it to him and he stuffed it in his pocket.

"I'll make it as brief as possible," Wolfe promised. "Harry Gould had an employer. One day he found a garage job-card in one of his employer's cars—possibly it had slipped under a seat and been forgotten—I don't know. Anyhow he found it and he kept it. I don't know why he kept it. He may have suspected that his employer had been on a trip with a woman, for the card was from a garage in Salamanca, New York, which is quite a distance from Long Island. A man with the blackmailing type of mind is apt to keep things. It is understandable that he kept the card. It is less understandable that his employer had been careless enough to leave it in the car." Wolfe turned his head suddenly and snapped at Hewitt:

"Was it just an oversight, Mr. Hewitt?"

But Hewitt had stuff in him at that. He was no longer pale and he wasn't licking his lips. His eyes were steady and so was his voice:

"Finish your story, Mr. Wolfe. I am inclined—but no matter. Finish your story."

"I prefer to use your name instead of clumsy circumlocutions like 'his employer.' It's neater."

"By all means keep it neat. But I warn you that merely because I acknowledged ownership of that cane—"

"Thank you. I appreciate warnings. So I'll say Hewitt hereafter. The time came when Harry Gould's suspicions regarding the card became more definite. Again I don't know why, but my surmise is that he learned about the loss of the most valuable plantation of broad-leaved evergreens in the country—the rhodalea plantation of the Updegraff Nurseries of Erie, Pennsylvania—by an attack of the Kurume yellows. He knew that Hewitt was inordinately proud of his own broad-leaved evergreens, and that he was capable of abnormal extremes in horticultural pride and jealousy. He also, being a gardener, knew how easy it would be, with a bag or two of contaminated peat mulch, to infect another plantation if you had access to it. At any rate, his suspicion became definite enough to cause him to go to Salamanca, which is in the western part of New York near the Pennsylvania border, not far from Erie, and see the proprietor of the Nelson Garage. That was in December. He learned that when Hewitt had gone there with his car months before, damaged in an accident, he had been accompanied not by a woman, but by a man of a certain description, with a cast in his eye. He went to Erie and found the man among the employees of the Updegraff Nurseries. His name was Pete Arango."

Fred Updegraff started up with an ejaculation.

Wolfe showed him a palm. "Please, Mr. Updegraff, don't prolong this." He turned. "And Mr. Hewitt, I'm being fair. I'm not trying to stampede you. I admit that much of this detail is surmise, but the main fact will soon be established beyond question. I sent a man to Salamanca last night, partly to learn why Harry Gould had so carefully preserved an old garage job-card, and partly because he had written on the back of it that name Pete Arango, and I knew that Pete Arango was in the employ of the Updegraff Nurseries. My man phoned me this morning to say that he will be back here at one o'clock, and the proprietor of the Nelson Garage will be with him. He'll tell us whether you were there with Pete Arango. Do you suppose you'll remember him?"

"I'll—" Hewitt swallowed. "Go ahead."

Wolfe nodded. "I imagine you will. I wouldn't be surprised if Gould even got a written confession from Pete Arango that you had bribed him to infect the rhodalea plantation, by threatening to inform Mr. Updegraff that he had been at Salamanca, not far away, in your company. At least he got something that served well enough to put the screws on you. You paid him something around five thousand dollars. Did he turn the confession over to you? I suppose so. And then—may I hazard a guess?"

"I think," Hewitt said evenly, "you've done too much guessing already."

"I'll try one more. Gould saw Pete Arango at the Flower Show, and the temptation was too much for him. He threatened him again, and made him sign another confession, and armed with that made another demand on you. What this time? Ten thousand? Twenty? Or he may even have got delusions of grandeur and gone to six figures. Anyhow, you saw that it couldn't go on. As long as ink and paper lasted for Pete Arango to write confessions with, you were hooked. So you—by the way, Mr. Updegraff, he's up there at your exhibit, isn't he, and available? Pete Arango? We'll want him when Mr. Nelson arrives."

"You're damn right he's available," Fred said grimly.

"Good."

Wolfe's head pivoted back to Hewitt. He paused, and the silence was heavy on us. He was timing his climax, and just to make it good he decorated it.

"I suppose," he said to Hewitt in a tone of doom, "you are familiar with the tradition of the drama? The three traditional knocks to herald the tragedy?"

He lifted the osmundine fork and brought it down again, thumping the floor with it, once, twice, thrice.

Hewitt gazed at him with a sarcastic smile, and it was a pretty good job with the smile.

"So," Wolfe said, "you were compelled to act, and you did so promptly and effectively. And skillfully, because, for instance, Mr. Cramer has apparently been unable to trace the revolver, and no man in the world is better at that sort of thing. As Honorary Chairman of the Committee, naturally you had the run of the exhibit floors at any hour of the day; I suppose you chose the morning, before the doors were opened to the public, to arrange that primitive apparatus. I don't pretend to be inside of your mind, so I don't know when or why you decided to use your own cane as the homicide bait for some unsuspecting passer-by. On the theory that—"

The door opened and Theodore Horstmann was on the threshold.

"Phone call for Mr. Hewitt," he said irritably. Theodore resented his work being interrupted by anything whatever. "Pete Arando or something?"

Hewitt stood up.

Cramer opened his mouth, but Wolfe beat him to it by saying sharply, "Wait! You'll stay here, Mr. Hewitt! Archie—no, I suppose he would recognize your voice. Yours too, Mr. Cramer. Mr. Dill. You can do it if you pitch your voice low. Lead him on, get him to say as much as you can—"

Hewitt said, "That phone call is for me," and was moving for the door. I got in front of him. Dill arose, looking uncertain.

"I don't know whether I can—"

"Certainly you can," Wolfe assured him. "Go ahead. The phone is there on the potting bench. Theodore, confound it, let him by and come in here and close the door."

Theodore obeyed orders. When Dill had passed through Theodore pulled the door shut and stood there resenting us. Hewitt sat down again and put his elbows on his knees and covered his face with his hands. Anne had her head turned not to look at him. That made her face Fred Updegraff, who was next to her, and I became aware for the first time that he was holding her hand. Hardly as private as in a taxi, but he had her hand.

"While we're waiting," Wolfe observed, "I may as well finish my speculations about the cane. Mr. Hewitt may have decided to use it on the theory that the fact of its being his cane would divert suspicion away from him instead of toward him. Was that it, Mr. Hewitt? But in that case, why did you submit to my threat to divulge the fact that it was your cane? I believe I can answer that too. Because you mistrusted my acumen? Because you were afraid my suspicions would be aroused if you failed to conform to the type of the eminent wealthy citizen zealously guarding his reputation from even the breath of scandal? Things like that gather complications as they go along. It's too bad."

Wolfe looked at Hewitt, and shook his head as though regretfully. "But I have no desire to torment you. Theodore, try the door."

"I don't have to," Theodore said, standing with his back to the door. "I heard the bolt. The lower one squeaks."

I stood up. Not that there was anything I intended to do or could do, but I was coming to in a rush and I couldn't stay sitting. Cramer did, but his eyes, on Wolfe, were nothing but narrow slits.

"Try it anyway," Wolfe said quietly.

Theodore turned and lifted the latch and pushed, and turned back again. "It's bolted."

"Indeed," Wolfe said with a tingle in his voice. His head turned. "Well, Miss Lasher, what do you think of it?" His eyes swept the faces. "I ask Miss Lasher because she knew all along that I was lying. She knew it couldn't have been Mr. Hewitt who put that cane there on the floor of the corridor, because she saw Mr. Dill do it. Mr. Hewitt, let me congratulate you on a superb performance—you can't force it, Mr. Cramer, it's a sturdy door—"

Cramer was at it, lifting the latch, assaulting the panel with his shoulder. He turned, his face purple, blurted, "By God, I might have known—," jumped across and grabbed up a heavy packing-box.

"Archie!" Wolfe called sharply.

In all my long and varied association with Inspector Cramer I had never had an opportunity to perform on him properly. This, at last, was it. I wrapped myself around him like cellophane around a toothbrush and turned on the pressure. For maybe five seconds he wriggled, and just as he stopped Fred Updegraff sprang to his feet and gasped in horror:

"Ciphogene! For God's sake—"

"Stop it!" Wolfe commanded. "I know what I'm doing! There is no occasion for panic. Mr. Cramer, there is an excellent reason why that door must not be opened. If Archie releases you, will you listen to it? No? Then, Archie, hold him. This is a fumigating room where we use ciphogene, a gas which will kill a man by asphyxiation in two minutes. The pipe runs from a tank in the potting room and the valve is in there. This morning I closed the outlet of the pipe in this room, and removed the plug from an outlet in the potting room. So if Mr. Dill has opened that valve in the potting room, he is dead, or soon will be. And if you batter a hole in that door I won't answer for the consequences. We might get out quickly enough and we might not."

"You goddamn balloon," Cramer sputtered helplessly. It was the first and only time I ever heard him cuss in the presence of ladies.

I unwrapped myself from him and stepped back. He shook himself and barked at Wolfe:

"Are you going to just sit there? Are we going to just sit here? Isn't there—can't you call someone—"

"I'll try," Wolfe said placidly. He lifted the osmundine fork and thumped the floor with it, five times, at regular intervals.

Lewis Hewitt murmured, believe it or not, apparently to Theodore, "I was in the dramatic club at college."

Chapter 10

"All right, I'll buy you a medal," Inspector Cramer said in utter disgust.

Five hours had passed. It was six thirty that evening, and the three of us were in the office. I was at my desk, Cramer was in the red leather chair, and Wolfe was seated behind his own desk, leaning back with his fingertips touching on top of his digestive domain. He looked a little creasy around the eyes, which were almost open.

Cramer went on sputtering: "Dill was a murderer, and he's dead, and you killed him. You maneuvered him into the potting room with a fake phone call, and he took the bait and bolted the door to the fumigating room and opened the valve. And then why didn't he walk out and go home? How did you know he wouldn't do that?"

"Pfui," Wolfe said lazily. He grunted. "Without waiting four minutes to make sure the ciphogene had worked? And leaving the door bolted, and the valve open? Mr. Dill was a fool, but not that big a fool. After a few minutes he would have closed the valve and opened the door, held his nose long enough to take a look at us and make sure we were finished, and departed, leaving the door closed but not bolted to give it the appearance of an accident. And probably leaving the valve a bit loose so it would leak a little." Wolfe grunted again. "No. That wasn't where the thin ice was. It was next thing to a certainty that Mr. Dill wouldn't decamp without having a look inside at us."

"You were sure of that."

"I was."

"You admit it."

"I do."

"Then you murdered him."

"My dear sir." Wolfe wiggled a finger in exasperation. "If you are privately branding me to relieve your feelings, I don't mind. If you are speaking officially, you are talking gibberish. I could be utterly candid even to a jury, regarding my preparations. I could admit that I plugged the outlet in the fumigating room, and opened the one in the potting room, so that it would be the latter, and not the former, that would be filled with ciphogene if Mr. Dill bolted that door and opened that valve. I could admit that I arranged with Mr. Hewitt to play his part, appealing to him in the interest of justice. He is a public-spirited man. And I discovered his weakness; he has always wanted to be an actor. He even gave me permission to mention his cane, and to recite that wild tale about him—which of course was true, though not true about him, but about Mr. Dill.

"I could admit that I arranged with Theodore also to play his part. He works for me and obeyed orders. I could admit that I had Fritz stationed in the room below, and my three thumps on the floor were a signal to him to make the telephone call for Mr. Hewitt, and the five thumps, later, told him to come upstairs and start the ventilating blowers in the potting room, which can be done from the hall. I could admit that I deliberately postponed the second signal to Fritz for three minutes after I learned that the door had been bolted; that I had previously released a minute quantity of ciphogene in the potting room and fumigating room so that Mr. Dill's nose would be accustomed to the smell and would not take alarm at any sudden odor in the potting room after he turned on the valve; that all my arrangements were made with the idea that if Mr. Dill should open that valve, thinking to murder all eight of us, he would die, I could admit all that to a jury."

Wolfe sighed. "But the fact would remain that Mr. Dill opened the valve of his own volition, intending to exterminate eight people, including you. No jury would find against me even for damage to your self-esteem."

"To hell with my self-esteem," Cramer growled. "Why don't you send a bill to the State of New York for the execution of a murderer f.o.b. your potting room? That's the only thing you've left out. Why don't you?"

Wolfe chuckled. "I wonder if I could collect. It's worth trying. I may tell you privately, Mr. Cramer, that there were several reasons why it would have been unfortunate for Mr. Dill to be brought to trial. One, it might have been difficult to convict him. Only a fairly good case. Two, the part played by Mr. Hewitt's cane would have been made public, and I had undertaken to prevent that. Three, Archie would have been embarrassed. He pulled the trigger and killed the man. Four, Miss Lasher would have committed suicide, or tried to. She's not very bright, but she's stubborn as the devil. She had decided that if she admitted having seen anything from her hiding-place in the corridor, she would have to testify to it publicly, her relations with Mr. Gould would have been exposed, and her family would have been dishonored."

"They would have been exposed anyway."

"Certainly, once you got hold of her. When Archie brought her to the potting room, with you there, she was a goner. That was the beauty of it. Mr. Dill knew she was bound to crack, and that coupled with the threat of being confronted with the garage man was what cracked him. It was a delicate situation. Among many others was the danger that during my recital Miss Lasher might blurt out that it was Dill, not Hewitt, who had placed the cane there by the door, and that would have spoiled everything."

"Wasn't it Hewitt's cane?"

"Yes. A fact as I have told you, not for publication."

"Where did Dill get it?"

"I don't know. Hewitt had mislaid it, and no doubt Dill spied it and decided to make use of it. By the way, another item not for publication is Miss Lasher's statement. Don't forget you promised that. I owe it to her. If she hadn't included that garage job-card when she packed Mr. Gould's belongings in her suitcase I wouldn't have got anywhere."

"And another thing," I put in. "A public airing of the little difficulty Miss Tracy's father got into wouldn't get you an increase in salary."

"Nothing in God's world would get me an increase in salary," Cramer declared feelingly. "And Miss Tracy's father—" He waved it away.

Wolfe's eyes came to me. "I thought you were no longer affianced to her."

"I'm not. But I'm sentimental about my memories. My lord, but she'll get sick of Fred. Peonies! Incidentally, while you're sweeping up, what was Annie's big secret?"

"Not so big." Wolfe glanced up at the clock, saw that it would be nearly an hour till dinner, and grimaced. "Miss Tracy admitted the soundness of my surmises this morning. Mr. Gould was as devious as he was ruthless. He told her that unless she married him he would force Mr. Dill to have her father arrested, and assured her that he had it in his power to do that. He also spoke of large sums of money. So naturally, when he was murdered Miss Tracy suspected that Mr. Dill was concerned in it, but she refused to disclose her suspicions for obvious reasons—the fear of consequences to her father."

Wolfe put his fingertips together again. "It is surprising that Mr. Gould lived as long as he did, in view of his character. He bragged to Miss Lasher that he was going to marry another girl. That was silly and sadistic. He let Miss Tracy know that he had a hold on Mr. Dill. That was rashly indiscreet. He even infected the Rucker and Dill exhibit with Kurume yellows, doubtless to dramatize the pressure he was exerting on Dill for his big haul—at least I presume he did. That was foolish and flamboyant. Of course Dill was equally foolish when he tried to engage me to investigate the Kurume yellows in his exhibit. He must have been unbalanced by the approaching murder he had arranged for, since bravado was not in his normal character. I suppose he had a hazy idea that hiring me to investigate in advance would help to divert suspicion from him. He really wasn't cut out for a murderer. His nerves weren't up to it."

"Yours are." Cramer stood up. "I've got to run. One thing I don't get, Dill's going clear to Pennsylvania to bribe a guy to poison some bushes. I know you spoke about extremes in horticultural jealousy, but have they all got it? Did Dill have it too?"

Wolfe shook his head. "I was then speaking of Mr. Hewitt. What Mr. Dill had was a desire to protect his investment and income. The prospect of those rhodaleas appearing on the market endangered the biggest department of his business." He suddenly sat up and spoke in a new tone. "But speaking of horticultural jealousy—I had a client, you know. I collected a fee in advance. I'd like to show it to you. Archie, will you bring them down, please?"

I was tired after all the hubbub and the strain of watching Wolfe through another of his little experiments, but he had said please, so I went up to the plant rooms and got them, all three of them, and brought them down and put them side by side on Wolfe's desk. He stood up and bent over them, beaming.

"They're absolutely unique," he said as if he was in church. "Matchless! Incomparable!"

"They're pretty," Cramer said politely, turning to go. "Kind of drab, though. Not much color. I like geraniums better."

That's the first of the two cases. That's how he got the black orchids. And what do you suppose he did with them? I don't mean the plants; it would take the lever Archimedes wanted a fulcrum for to pry one of those plants loose from him (just last week Cuyler Ditson offered him enough for one to buy an antiaircraft gun); I mean a bunch of the blossoms. I saw them myself there on a corner of the casket, with a card he had scribbled his initials on, "N.W." That was all.

I put this case here with the other one only on account of the orchids. As I said, it's a totally different set of people. If, when you finish it, you think the mystery has been solved, all I have to say is you don't know a mystery when you see one.

A. G.

CORDIALLY INVITED TO MEET DEATH

Chapter 1

That wasn't the first time I ever saw Bess Huddleston.

A couple of years previously she had phoned the office one afternoon and asked to speak to Nero Wolfe, and when Wolfe got on the wire she calmly requested him to come at once to her place up at Riverdale to see her. Naturally he cut her off short. In the first place, he never stirred out of the house except in the direction of an old friend or a good cook; and secondly, it hurt his vanity that there was any man or woman alive who didn't know that.

An hour or so later here she came, to the office—the room he used for an office in his old house on West 35th Street, near the river—and there was a lively fifteen minutes. I never saw him more furious. It struck me as an attractive proposition. She offered him two thousand bucks to come to a party she was arranging for a Mrs. Somebody and be the detective in a murder game. Only four or five hours' work, sitting down, all the beer he could drink, and two thousand dollars. She even offered an extra five hundred for me to go along and do the leg work. But was he outraged! You might have thought he was Napoleon and she was asking him to come and deploy the tin soldiers in a nursery.

After she had gone I deplored his attitude. I told him that after all she was nearly as famous as he was, being the most successful party-arranger for the upper brackets that New York had ever had, and a combination of the talents of two such artists as him and her would have been something to remember, not to mention what I could do in the way of fun with five hundred smackers, but all he did was sulk.

That had been two years before. Now, this hot August morning with no air conditioning in the house because he distrusted machinery, she phoned around noon and asked him to come up to her place at Riverdale right away. He motioned to me to dispose of her and hung up. But a little later, when he had gone to the kitchen to consult with Fritz about some problem that had arisen in connection with lunch, I looked up her number and called her back. It had been as dull as a blunt instrument around the office for nearly a month, ever since we had finished with the Nauheim case, and I would have welcomed even tailing a laundry boy suspected of stealing a bottle of pop, so I phoned and told her that if she was contemplating a trip to 35th Street I wanted to remind her that Wolfe was incommunicado upstairs with his orchid plants from nine to eleven in the morning, and from four to six in the afternoon, but that any other time he would be delighted to see her.

I must say he didn't act delighted, when I ushered her in from the hall around three o'clock that afternoon. He didn't even apologize for not getting up from his chair to greet her, though I admit no reasonable person would have expected any such effort after one glance at his dimensions.

"You," he muttered pettishly, "are the woman who came here once and tried to bribe me to play the clown."

She plopped into the red leather chair I placed for her,

got a handkerchief out of her large green handbag, and passed it across her forehead, the back of her neck, and her throat. She was one of those people who don't look much like their pictures in the paper, because her eyes made her face and made you forget the rest of it when you looked at her. They were black and bright and gave you the feeling they were looking at you when they couldn't have been, and they made her seem a lot younger than the forty-seven or forty-eight she probably was.

"My God," she said, "as hot as this I should think you would sweat more. I'm in a hurry because I've got to see the Mayor about a Defense Pageant he wants me to handle, so I haven't time to argue, but your saying I tried to bribe you is perfectly silly. Perfectly silly! It would have been a marvelous party with you for the detective, but I had to get a policeman, an inspector, and all he did was grunt. Like this." She grunted.

"If you have come, madam, to—"

"I haven't. I don't want you for a party this time. I wish I did. Someone is trying to ruin me."

"Ruin you? Physically, financially—"

"Just ruin me. You know what I do. I do parties—"

"I know what you do," Wolfe said curtly.

"Very well. My clients are rich people and important people, at least they think they're important. Without going into that, they're important to me. So what do you suppose the effect would be—wait, I'll show it to you—"

She opened her handbag and dug into it like a terrier. A small bit of paper fluttered to the floor, and I stepped across to retrieve it for her, but she darted a glance at it and said, "Don't bother, wastebasket," and I disposed of it as indicated and returned to my chair.

Bess Huddleston handed an envelope to Wolfe. "Look at that. What do you think of that?"

Wolfe looked at the envelope, front and back, took

from it a sheet of paper which he unfolded and looked at, and passed them over to me.

"This is confidential," Bess Huddleston said.

"So is Mr. Goodwin," Wolfe said dryly.

I examined the exhibits. The envelope, stamped and postmarked and slit open, was addressed on a typewriter:

Mrs. Jervis Horrocks
902 East 74th Street
New York City

The sheet of paper said, also typewritten:

Was it ignorance or something else that caused Dr. Brady to prescribe the wrong medicine for your daughter? Ask Bess Huddleston. She can tell you if she will. She told me.

There was no signature. I handed the sheet and envelope back to Wolfe.

Bess Huddleston used her handkerchief on her forehead and throat again. "There was another one," she said, looking at Wolfe but her eyes making me feel she was looking at me, "but I haven't got it. That one, as you see, is postmarked Tuesday, August 12th, six days ago. The other one was mailed a day earlier, Monday, the 11th, a week ago today. Typewritten, just like that. I've seen it. It was sent to a very rich and prominent man, and it said—I'll repeat it. It said: 'Where and with whom does your wife spend most of her afternoons? If you knew you would be surprised. My authority for this is Bess Huddleston. Ask her.' The man showed it to me. His wife is one of my best—"

"Please." Wolfe wiggled a finger at her. "Are you consulting me or hiring me?"

"I'm hiring you. To find out who sent those things."

"It's a mean kind of a job. Often next to impossible. Nothing but greed could induce me to tackle it."

"Certainly." Bess Huddleston nodded impatiently. "I know how to charge too. I expect to get soaked. But where will I be if this isn't stopped and stopped quick?"

"Very well. Archie, your notebook."

I got it out and got busy. She reeled it off to me while Wolfe rang for beer and then leaned back and closed his eyes. But he opened one of them halfway when he heard her telling me about the stationery and the typewriter. The paper and envelopes of both the anonymous letters, she said, were the kind used for personal correspondence by a girl who worked for her as her assistant in party-arranging, named Janet Nichols; and the letters and envelopes had been typed on a typewriter that belonged to Bess Huddleston herself which was used by another girl who worked for her as her secretary, named Maryella Timms. Bess Huddleston had done no comparing with a magnifying glass, but it looked like the work of that typewriter. Both girls lived with her in her house at Riverdale, and there was a large box of that stationery in Janet Nichols' room.

Then if not one of the girls—one of the girls? Wolfe muttered, "Facts, Archie." Servants? No use to bother about the servants, Bess Huddleston said; no servant ever stayed with her long enough to develop a grudge. I passed it with a nod having read about the alligators and bears and other disturbing elements in newspaper and magazine pieces. Did anyone else live in the house? Yes, a nephew, Lawrence Huddleston, also on the payroll as an assistant party-arranger, but, according to Aunt Bess, not on any account to be suspected. That all? Yes. Any persons sufficiently intimate with the household to have had access to the typewriter and Janet Nichols' stationery?

Certainly, as possibilities, many people.

Wolfe grunted impolitely. I asked, for another fact, what about the insinuations in the anonymous letters? The wrong medicine and the questionable afternoons? Bess Huddleston's black eyes snapped at me. She knew nothing about those things. And anyway, they were irrelevant. The point was that some malicious person was trying to ruin her by spreading hints that she was blabbing guilty secrets about people, and whether the secrets happened to be true or not had nothing to do with it. Okay, I told her, forget about where Mrs. Rich Man spends her afternoons, maybe at the ball game, but as a matter of record did Mrs. Jervis Horrocks have a daughter, and had she been sick, and had Dr. Brady attended her? Yes, Bess Huddleston said impatiently, Mrs. Horrocks' daughter had died a month ago and Dr. Brady had been her doctor. Died of what? Tetanus. How had she got tetanus? By scratching her arm on a nail in a riding-academy stable.

Wolfe muttered, "There is no wrong medicine—"

"It was terrible," Bess Huddleston interrupted, "but it has nothing to do with this. I'm going to be late for my appointment with the Mayor. This is perfectly simple. Someone wanted to ruin me and conceived this filthy way of doing it, that's all. It has to be stopped, and if you're as smart as you're supposed to be, you can stop it. Of course, I ought to tell you, I know who did it."

I cocked my head at her. Wolfe's eyes opened wide.

"What? You know?"

"Yes, I think I know. No, I do know."

"Then why, madam, are you annoying me?"

"Because I can't prove it. And she denies it."

"Indeed." Wolfe shot a sharp glance at her. "You seem to be less intelligent than you look. If, having no proof, you charged her with it."

"Did I say charged her with it? I didn't. I discussed it

with her, and also with Maryella, and my nephew, and Dr. Brady, and my brother. I asked them questions. I saw I couldn't handle it. So I came to you."

"By elimination—the culprit is Miss Nichols."

"Yes."

Wolfe was frowning. "But you have no proof. What do you have?"

"I have—a feeling."

"Pfui. Based on what?"

"I know her."

"You do." Wolfe continued to frown, and his lips pushed out, once, and in again. "By divination? Phrenology? What specific revelations of her character have you observed? Does she pull chairs from under people?"

"Cut the glitter," Bess Huddleston snapped, frowning back at him. "You know quite well what I mean. I say I know her, that's all. Her eyes, her voice, her manner—"

"I see. Flatly, you don't like her. She must be either remarkably stupid or extremely clever, to have used her own stationery for anonymous letters. Had you thought of that?"

"Certainly. She is clever."

"But knowing she did this, you keep her in your employ, in your house?"

"Of course I do. If I discharged her, would that stop her?"

"No. But you say you think her guilty because you know her. That means you knew a week ago, a month ago, a year ago that she was the sort of person who would do this sort of thing. Why didn't you get rid of her?"

"Because I—" Bess Huddleston hesitated. "What difference does that make?" she demanded.

"It makes a big difference to me, madam. You've hired me to investigate the source of those letters. I am doing so now. I am considering the possibility that you sent them yourself."

Her eyes flashed at him. "I? Nonsense."

"Then answer me." Wolfe was imperturbable. "Since you knew what Miss Nichols was like, why didn't you fire her?"

"Because I needed her. She's the best assistant I've ever had. Her ideas are simply . . . take the Stryker dwarf and giant party . . . that was her idea . . . this is confidential . . . some of my biggest successes . . ."

"I see. How long has she worked for you?"

"Three years."

"Do you pay her adequately?"

"Yes. I didn't, but I do now. Ten thousand a year."

"Then why does she want to ruin you? Just cussedness? Or has she got it in for you?"

"She has—she thinks she has a grievance."

"What about?"

"Something . . ." Bess Huddleston shook her head. "That's of no importance. A private matter. It wouldn't help you any. I am willing to pay your bill for finding out who sent those letters and getting proof."

"You mean you will pay me for fastening the guilt on Miss Nichols."

"Not at all. On whoever did it."

"No matter who it is?"

"Certainly."

"But you're sure it's Miss Nichols."

"I am not sure. I said I have a feeling." Bess Huddleston stood up and picked up her handbag from Wolfe's desk. "I have to go. Can you come up to my place tonight?"

"No. Mr.—"

"When can you come?"

"I can't. Mr. Goodwin can go—" Wolfe stopped himself. "No. Since you have already discussed it with all of those people, I'd like to see them. First the young women. Send them down here. I'll be free at six o'clock. This is a nasty job and I want to get it over with."

"My God," Bess Huddleston said, her eyes snapping at him, "you would have made a wonderful party! If I could sell it to the Crowthers I could make it four thousand—only there won't be many more parties for me if we don't get these letters stopped. I'll phone the girls—"

"Here's a phone," I said.

She made the call, gave instructions to one she called Maryella, and departed in a rush.

When I returned to the office after seeing the visitor to the door, Wolfe was out of his chair. There was nothing alarming about that, since it was one minute to four and therefore time for him to go up to the orchids, but what froze me in my tracks was the sight of him stooping over, actually bending nearly double, with his hand in my wastebasket.

He straightened up.

"Did you hurt yourself?" I inquired anxiously.

Ignoring that, he moved nearer the window to inspect an object he held between his thumb and forefinger. I stepped over and he handed it to me and I took a squint at it. It was a snapshot of a girl's face, nothing special to my taste, trimmed off so it was six-sided in shape and about the size of a half dollar.

"Want it for your album?" I asked him.

He ignored that too. "There is nothing in the world," he said, glaring at me as if I had sent him an anonymous letter, "as indestructible as human dignity. That woman makes money killing time for fools. With it she pays me for rooting around in mud. Half of my share goes for taxes which are used to make bombs to blow people to pieces. Yet I am not without dignity. Ask Fritz, my cook. Ask Theodore, my gardener. Ask you, my—"

"Right hand."

"No."

"Prime minister."

"No."

"Pal."

"No!"

"Accomplice, flunkey, Secretary of War, hireling, comrade . . ." He was on his way out to the elevator. I tossed the snapshot onto my desk and went to the kitchen for a glass of milk.

Chapter 2

"You're late," I told the girls reproachfully as I showed them into the office. "Mr. Wolfe supposed you would be here at six o'clock, when he comes down from the plant rooms, and it's twenty after. Now he's gone to the kitchen and started operations on some corned beef hash."

They were sitting down and I was looking them over.

"You mean he's eating corned beef hash?" Maryella Timms asked.

"No. That comes later. He's concocting it."

"It's my fault," Janet Nichols said. "I didn't get back until after five, and I was in riding clothes and had to change. I'm sorry."

She didn't look much like a horseback rider. Not that she was built wrong, she had a fairly nice little body, with good hips, but her face was more of a subway face than a bridle-path face. Naturally I had been expecting something out of the ordinary, one way or another, since according to Bess Huddleston she was an anonymous letter writer and had thought up the Stryker dwarf and giant party, and to tell the truth I was disappointed. She looked more like a school teacher—or maybe it would be more accurate to say that she looked like what a school teacher looks like before the time comes that she absolutely looks like a school teacher and nothing else.

Maryella Timms, on the other hand, was in no way disappointing, but she was irritating. Her hair started far back above the slant of her brow, and that made her brow look even higher and broader than it was, and noble and spiritual. But her eyes were very demure, which didn't fit. If you're noble and spiritual you don't have to be demure. There's no point in being demure unless there's something on your mind to be demure about. Besides, there was her accent. Cawned beef ha-a-sh. I am not still fighting the Civil War, and anyway my side won, but these Southern belles—if it sounds like a deliberate come-on to me then it does. I was bawn and braht up in the Nawth.

"I'll see if I can pry him loose," I said, and went to the hall and through to the kitchen.

The outlook was promising for getting Wolfe to come and attend to business, because he had not yet got his hands in the hash. The mixture, or the start of it, was there in a bowl on the long table, and Fritz, at one side of the table, and Wolfe, at the other, were standing there discussing it. They looked around at me as I would expect to be looked at if I busted into a Cabinet meeting at the White House.

"They're here," I announced. "Janet and Maryella."

From the expression on his face as his mouth opened it was a safe bet that Wolfe was going to instruct me to tell them to come back tomorrow, but he didn't get it out. I heard a door open behind me and a voice floated past:

"Ah heah yawl makin' cawned beef ha-a-sh. . . ."

That's the last time I try to reproduce it.

The owner of the voice floated past me too, right up beside Wolfe. She leaned over to peer into the bowl.

"Excuse me," she said, which I couldn't spell the way

she said it anyhow, "but corned beef hash is one of my specialties. Nothing in there but meat, is there?"

"As you see," Wolfe grunted.

"It's ground too fine," Maryella asserted.

Wolfe scowled at her. I could see he was torn with conflicting emotions. A female in his kitchen was an outrage. A woman criticizing his or Fritz's cooking was an insult. But corned beef hash was one of life's toughest problems, never yet solved by anyone. To tone down the corned flavor and yet preserve its unique quality, to remove the curse of its dryness without making it greasy—the theories and experiments had gone on for years. He scowled at her, but he didn't order her out.

"This is Miss Timms," I said. "Mr. Wolfe. Mr. Brenner. Miss Nichols is in—"

"Ground too fine for what?" Wolfe demanded truculently. "This is not a tender fresh meat, with juices to lose—"

"Now you just calm down." Maryella's hand was on his arm. "It's not ruined, only it's better if it's coarser. That's far too much potatoes for that meat. But if you don't have chitlins you can't—"

"Chitlins!" Wolfe bellowed.

Maryella nodded. "Fresh pig chitlins. That's the secret of it. Fried shallow in olive oil with onion juice—"

"Good heavens!" Wolfe was staring at Fritz. "I never heard of it. It has never occurred to me. Fritz? Well?"

Fritz was frowning thoughtfully. "It might go," he conceded. "We can try it. As an experiment."

Wolfe turned to me in swift decision. "Archie, call up Kretzmeyer and ask if he has pig chitlins. Two pounds."

"You'd better let me help," Maryella said. "It's sort of tricky. . . ."

That was how I came to get so well acquainted with Janet that first day. I thought I might as well have company driving down to the market for chitlins, and Maryella was glued to Wolfe, and as far as that's concerned Wolfe was glued to her for the duration of the experiment, so I took Janet along. By the time we got back to the house I had decided she was innocent in more ways than one, though I admit that didn't mean much, because it's hard for me to believe that anyone not obviously a hyena could pull a trick like anonymous letters. I also admit there wasn't much sparkle to her, and she seemed to be a little absent-minded when it came to conversation, but under the circumstances that wasn't surprising, if she knew why she had been told to go to Nero Wolfe's office, as she probably did.

I delivered the chitlins to the hash artists in the kitchen and then joined Janet in the office. I had been telling her about orchid hybridizing on the way back uptown, and when I went to my desk to get a stack of breeding cards I was going to show her, I noticed something was missing. So I gave her the cards to look at and excused myself and returned to the kitchen, and asked Wolfe if anyone had been in the office during my absence. He was standing beside Maryella, watching Fritz arrange the chitlins on a cutting board, and all I got was a growl.

"None of you left the kitchen?" I insisted.

"No," he said shortly. "Why?"

"Someone ate my lollipop," I told him, and left him with his playmates and returned to the office. Janet was sitting with the cards in her lap, going through them. I stood in front of her and inquired amiably:

"What did you do with it?"

She looked up at me. That way, with her head tilted up, from that angle, she looked kind of pretty.

"What did I—what?"

"That snapshot you took from my desk. It's the only picture I've got of you. Where did you put it?"

"I didn't—" Her mouth closed. "I didn't!" she said defiantly.

I sat down and shook my head at her. "Now listen," I said pleasantly. "Don't lie to me. We're comrades. Side by side we have sought the chitlin in its lair. The wild boar chitlin. That picture is my property and I want it. Let's say it fluttered into your bag. Look in your bag."

"It isn't there." With a new note of spunk in her voice, and a new touch of color on her cheeks, she was more of a person. Her bag was beside her on the chair, and her left hand was clutching it.

"Then I'll look in your bag." I started for her.

"No!" she said. "It isn't there!" She put a palm to her stomach. "It's here."

I stopped short, thinking for a second she had swallowed it. Then I returned to my chair and told her, "Okay. You will now return it. You have three alternatives. Either dig it out yourself, or I will, or I'll call in Maryella and hold you while she does. The first is the most ladylike. I'll turn my back."

"Please." She kept her palm against her stomach. "Please! It's my picture!"

"It's a picture of you, but it's not your picture."

"Miss Huddleston gave it to you."

I saw no point in denying the obvious. "Say she did."

"And she told you . . . she . . . she thinks I sent those awful letters! I know she does!"

"That," I said firmly, "is another matter which the boss is handling. I am handling the picture. It is probably of no importance except as a picture of the girl who thought up the Stryker dwarf and giant party. If you ask Mr. Wolfe for it he'll probably give it to you. It may even be that Miss Huddleston stole it; I don't know. She didn't say where she got it. I do know that you copped it from my desk and I want it back. You can get another one, but I can't. Shall I call Maryella?" I turned my head and looked like a man about to let out a yell.

"No!" she said, and got out of her chair and turned her back and went through some contortions. When she handed me the snapshot I tucked it under a paperweight on Wolfe's desk and then went to help her collect the breeding cards from the floor where they had tumbled from her lap.

"Look what you did," I told her, "mixed them all up. Now you can help me put them in order again. . . ."

It looked for a minute as if tears were going to flow, but they didn't. We spent an hour together, not exactly jolly, but quite friendly. I avoided the letter question, because I didn't know what line Wolfe intended to take.

When he finally got at it there was no line to it. That was after nine o'clock, when we assembled in the office after the hash and trimmings had been disposed of. The hash was okay. It was good hash. Wolfe had three helpings, and when he conversed with Maryella, as he did through most of the meal, he was not only sociable but positively respectful. There was an unpleasant moment at the beginning, when Janet didn't take any hash and Fritz was told to slice some ham for her, and Maryella told her resentfully:

"You won't eat it because I cooked it."

Janet protested that that wasn't so, she just didn't like corned beef.

In the office, afterwards, it became apparent that there was no love lost between the secretary and the assistant party-arranger. Not that either accused the other of writing the poison-pen letters; there were no open hostilities, but a few glances I observed when I looked up from my notebook, and tones of voice when they addressed each other, sounded as if there might be quite a blaze if somebody touched a match to it. Wolfe didn't get anything, as far as I could see, except a collection of unimportant facts. Both the girls were being discreet, to put it mildly. Bess Huddleston, according to them, was a very satisfactory employer. They admitted that her celebrated eccentricities made things difficult sometimes, but they had no kick coming. Janet had worked for her three years, and Maryella two, and they hadn't the slightest idea who could have sent those dreadful letters, and Bess Huddleston had no enemies that they knew of . . . oh, of course, she had hurt some people's feelings, but what did that amount to, and there were scores of people who could have got at Janet's stationery during the past months but they couldn't imagine who, and so forth and so on. Yes, they had known Mrs. Jervis Horrocks' daughter, Helen; she had been a close friend of Maryella's. Her death had been a shock. And yes, they knew Dr. Alan Brady quite well. He was fashionable and successful and had a wonderful reputation for his age. He often went horseback riding with one of them or with Bess Huddleston. Riding academy? No, Bess Huddleston kept horses in her stable at her place at Riverdale, and Dr. Brady would come up from the Medical Center when he got through in the afternoon—it was only a ten-minute drive.

And Bess Huddleston had never been married, and her brother Daniel was some kind of a chemist, not in society, very much not, who showed up at the house for dinner about once a week; and her nephew, Larry, well, there he was, that was all, a young man living there and getting paid for helping his aunt in her business; and there were no other known relatives and no real intimates, except that Bess Huddleston had hundreds of intimates of both sexes and all ages. . . .

It went on for nearly two hours.

After seeing them out to their car—I noticed Maryella was driving—I returned to the office and stood and watched Wolfe down a glass of beer and pour another one.

"That picture of the culprit," I said, "is there under your paperweight if you want it. She did. I mean she wanted it. In my absence she swiped it and hid it in a spot too intimate to mention in your presence. I got it back—no matter how. I expected her to ask you for it, but she didn't. And if you think you're going to solve this case by—"

"Confound the case." Wolfe sighed clear to the beer he had swallowed. "I might have known better. Tomorrow go up there and look around. The servants, I suppose. Make sure of the typewriter. The nephew. Talk with him and decide if I must see him; if so, bring him. And get Dr. Brady here. After lunch would be best."

"Sure," I said sarcastically.

"Around two o'clock. Please get your notebook and take a letter. Get it off tonight, special delivery. To Professor Martingale of Harvard. Dear Joseph. I have made a remarkable discovery, comma, or rather, comma, have had one communicated to me. You may remember our discussion last winter regarding the possibility of using pig chitlins in connection with . . ."

Chapter 3

Ever since an incident that occurred when Wolfe sent me on an errand in February, 1935, I automatically ask myself, when leaving the office on a business chore, do I take a gun? I seldom do; but if I had done so that Tuesday afternoon I swear I would have found use for it. As sure as my name is Archie and not Archibald, I would have shot that goddamn orangutan dead in his tracks.

Formerly it took a good three-quarters of an hour to drive from 35th Street to Riverdale, but now, with the West Side Highway and the Henry Hudson Bridge, twenty minutes was ample. I had never seen the Huddleston place before, but since I read newspapers and magazines the trick fence was no surprise to me. I parked the roadster at a wide space on the drive which ran parallel with the fence, got a gate open and went through, and started up a path across the lawn towards the house. There were trees and bushes around, and off to the right an egg-shaped pool.

About twenty paces short of the house I suddenly stopped. I don't know where he had appeared from, but there he was straddling the path, big and black, his teeth flashing in a grin if you want to call it that. I stood and looked at him. He didn't move. I thought to myself, nuts, and moved forward, but when I got closer he made a certain kind of a noise and I stopped again. Okay, I thought, if this is your private path why didn't you say so, and I sashayed off to the right, seeing there was another path the other side of the pool. I didn't actually turn but went sort of sidewise because I was curious to see what he was going to do, and what he did was stalk me, on all fours. So it happened that my head was twisted to keep an eye on him when I backed into a log there on the grass at the edge of the pool and went down flat, nearly tumbling into the water, and when I sprang to my feet again the log was crawling along the ground length-wise towards me. It was one of the alligators. The orangutan was sitting down laughing. I don't mean he was making a laughing noise, but by his face he was laughing. That's when I would have shot him. I circled around the pool and got to the other path and headed for the house, but there he was, straddling the path ten yards ahead of me, making the noise again, so I stopped.

A man's voice said, "He wants to play tag."

I had been too preoccupied to see the man, and anyway he had just stepped from behind a shrub at the end of a terrace. With a glance I saw that he was clad in a green shirt and brick-colored slacks, was about my age or a little younger, and seemed to be assuming a supercilious attitude.

He said, "He wants to play tag."

I said, "I don't."

He said, "If you offend him he'll bite you. Start past him on the grass and dodge when he goes to touch you. Dodge three times and then let him tag you, and say 'Mister' in an admiring voice. That's all. His name is Mister."

"I could turn around and go home."

"I wouldn't try that. He would resent it."

"I could sock him one."

"You might. I doubt it. If you hurt him and my aunt ever catches you . . . I suppose you're Archie Goodwin? I'm Larry Huddleston. I didn't send those letters and don't know who did or who might. My aunt will be down later, she's upstairs arguing with Brother Daniel. I can't invite you in until you get past Mister."

"Does everyone who comes here have to play tag with this damn overgrown orangutan?"

"He's not an orangutan; he's a chimpanzee. He doesn't often play with strangers. It means he likes you."

I had to go through with it. I took to the grass, was intercepted, dodged three times, said 'Mister' in as admiring a tone of voice as I could manage, and was by. Mister emitted a little squeal and scampered off to a tree and bounded up to a limb. I looked at the back of my hand and saw blood. The nephew asked, not with great concern:

"Did he bite you?"

"No, I fell down and must have scratched it. It's just a scratch."

"Yeah, I saw you trip over Moses. I'll get you some iodine."

I said it wasn't worth bothering about, but he took me across the terrace into the house, into a large living room, twice as long as it was broad, with big windows and a big fireplace, and enough chairs and divans and cushions for a good-sized party right there. When he opened a cupboard door in the wall near the fireplace a shelf was disclosed with a neat array of sterilized gauze, band-aids, adhesive tape, and salve. . . .

As I dabbed iodine on the scratch I said, for something to say, "Handy place for a first-aid outfit."

He nodded. "On account of Mister. He never bites

deep, but he often breaks somebody's skin. Then Logo and Lulu, sometimes they take a little nip—"

"Logo and Lulu?"

"The bears."

"Oh, sure. The bears." I looked around and then put the iodine bottle on the shelf and he closed the door. "Where are they now?"

"Having a nap somewhere. They always nap in the afternoon. They'll be around later. Shall we go out to the terrace? What'll you have, scotch, rye, bourbon?"

It was a nice spot, the terrace, on the shady side of the house with large irregular flagstones separated by ribbons of turf. I sat there for an hour with him, but about all I got out of it was three highballs. I didn't cotton to him much. He talked like an actor; he had a green handkerchief in the breast pocket of his shirt, to match the shirt; he mentioned the Social Register three times in less than an hour; and he wore an hexagonal wrist watch, whereas there's no excuse for a watch to be anything but round. He struck me as barely bright enough for life's simplest demands, but I admit he might have been a darb at a party. I must say he didn't turn loose any secrets. He was pretty indignant about the letters, but about all I learned from him was that he knew how to use a typewriter, that Maryella had gone downtown on some errands, and that Janet was out horseback riding with Dr. Brady. He seemed to be a little cynical about Dr. Brady, but I couldn't get the slant.

When it got five o'clock and his aunt hadn't come down, he went to inquire, and in a moment returned and said I was to go up. He led me upstairs and showed me a door and beat it. I entered and found I was in an office, but there was no one there. It was a mess. Phone books were heaped on a chair. The blotters had been used since the Declaration of Independence. The typewriter wasn't covered. I was frowning around when I heard steps, and Bess Huddleston trotted in, with a skinny specimen behind her. His eyes were as black as hers, but everything else about him was shrunk and faded. As she breezed past me she said:

"Sorry. How are you. My brother. Mr. Goldwyn."

"Goodwin," I said firmly, and shook brother's hand. I was surprised to find he had a good shake. Sister was sitting at a desk, opening a drawer. She got out a checkbook, took a pen from a socket, made out a check, tried to blot it and made a smudge, and handed it to brother Daniel. He took one look at it and said:

"No."

"Yes," she snapped.

"I tell you, Bess, it won't—"

"It will have to, Dan. At least for this week. That's all there is to it. I've told you a thousand times—"

She stopped, looked at me, and looked at him.

"All right," he said, and stuck the check in his pocket, and sat down on a chair, shaking his head and looking thoughtful.

"Now," Bess turned to me, "what about it?"

"Nothing to brag about," I told her. "There's a slew of fingerprints on that letter and envelope, but since you discussed it with your brother and nephew and the girls and Dr. Brady, I suppose they all handled it. Did they?"

"Yes."

I shrugged. "So. Maryella showed Mr. Wolfe how to make corned beef hash. The secret is chitlins. Aside from that, nothing to report. Except that Janet knows that you think she's it. Also she wanted that picture."

"What picture?"

"The snapshot of her you told me to throw in the wastebasket. It caught her eye and she wanted it. Is there any objection to her having it?"

"Certainly not."

"Is there anything you want to say about it? That might help?"

"No, that picture has nothing to do with it. I mean that wouldn't help you any."

"Dr. Brady was requested to call at our office at two o'clock today but was too busy."

Bess Huddleston went to a window and looked out and came back. "He wasn't too busy to come and ride one of my horses," she said tartly. "They ought to be back soon—I thought I heard them at the stable. . . ."

"Will he come to the house?"

"He will. For cocktails."

"Good. Mr. Wolfe told me to say that there is a remote chance there might be prints on the other letter. The one the rich man got."

"It isn't available."

"Couldn't you get it?"

"I don't think so."

"Has he turned it over to the police?"

"Good heavens, no!"

"Okay. I've played tag with Mister and had a talk with your nephew. Now if I could see where Janet keeps her stationery, and take a sample from that typewriter. Is that the one?"

"Yes. But first come to Janet's room. I'll show you."

I followed her. It was at the other end of the house, on that floor, one flight up, a pleasant little room and nice and neat. But the stationery was a washout. It wasn't in a box. It was in a drawer of a writing table with no lock on it, and all you had to do was open the drawer with a metal ring for a puller, which couldn't possibly have had a print, and reach in and take what you wanted, paper and envelopes both. Bess Huddleston left me there, and after a look around where there was nothing to look for, I went back to the office. Daniel was still there on the chair where we had left him. I ran off some sample lines on the typewriter, using a sheet of Janet's paper, and was putting it in my pocket when Daniel spoke:

"You're a detective."

I nodded. "That's what they tell me."

"You're finding out who sent those anonymous letters."

"Right." I snapped my fingers. "Just like that."

"Anyone who sends letters like that deserves to be immersed to the chin in a ten percent solution of hydrofluoric acid."

"Why, would that be painful?"

Daniel shuddered. "It would. I stayed here because I thought you might want to ask me something."

"Much obliged. What shall I ask you?"

"That's the trouble." He looked dismal. "There's nothing I can tell you. I wish to God there was. I have no information to offer, even no suspicions. But I would like to offer a comment. Without prejudice. Two comments."

I sat down and looked interested. "Number one?" I said receptively.

"You can pass them on to Nero Wolfe."

"I can and will."

Daniel eyed me, screwing up his lips. "You mentioned five people to my sister just now. Her nephew, Larry—mine too—Miss Nichols and Miss Timms, Dr. Brady, and me. It is worth considering that four of us would be injured by anything that injured my sister. I am her brother and I have a deep and strong affection for her. The young ladies are employed by her and they are well paid. Larry is also well paid. Frankly—I am his uncle—too well. But for his aunt, he might earn four dollars a day as a helper on a coal barge. I know of no other occupation that would not strain his faculties beyond their limit. But the point is, his prosperity depends entirely on hers. So it is conceivable—I offer this merely as a comment—that we four may properly be eliminated from suspicion."

"Okay," I said. "That leaves one."

"One?"

"Sure, Doc Brady. Of the five I mentioned, you rule out four. Pointing straight at him."

"By no means." Daniel looked distressed. "You misunderstand me. I know very little about Dr. Brady, though it so happens that my second comment concerns him. I insist it is merely a comment. You have read the letter received by Mrs. Horrocks? Then you have probably realized that while it purports to be an attack on Dr. Brady, it is so manifestly absurd that it couldn't possibly damage him. Mrs. Horrocks' daughter died of tetanus. There is no such thing as a wrong medicine for tetanus, nor a right one either, once the toxin has reached the nerve centers. The antitoxin will prevent, but never, or very rarely, will it cure. So the attack on Dr. Brady was no attack at all."

"That's interesting," I admitted. "Are you a doctor?"

"No, sir. I'm a research chemist. But any standard medical treatise—"

"Sure. I'll look it up. What reason do you suppose Doc Brady might have for putting your sister on the skids?"

"So far as I know, none. None whatever."

"Then that lets him out. With everyone else out, there's no one left but your sister."

"My sister?"

I nodded. "She must have sent the letters herself."

That made him mad. In fact he rather blew up, chiefly because it was too serious a matter to be facetious about, and I had to turn on the suavity to calm him down. Then he went into a sulk. After fooling around with him for another ten minutes and getting nothing for my trouble, I decided to move on and he accompanied me downstairs and out to the terrace, where we heard voices.

If that was a sample of a merry gathering arranged by Bess Huddleston, I'll roll my own, though I admit that isn't fair, since she hadn't done any special arranging. She was lying on a porch swing with her dress curled above her knees by the breeze, displaying a pair of bare legs that were merely something to walk with, the feet being shod with high-heeled red slippers, and I don't like shoes without stockings, no matter whose legs they are. Two medium-sized black bears were sitting on the flagstones with their backs propped against the frame of the swing, licking sticks of candy and growling at each other. Maryella Timms was perched on the arm of a chair with her hand happening to rest on the shoulder of Larry Huddleston, who was sitting at careless ease in the chair the way John Barrymore would. Janet Nichols, in riding clothes, was in another chair, her face hot and flushed, which made her look better instead of worse as it does most people, and standing at the other end of the swing, also in riding clothes, was a wiry-looking guy with a muscular face.

When Bess Huddleston introduced us, Dr. Brady and me, I started to meet him halfway for the handshake, but I had taken only two and a half steps when the bears suddenly started for me as if I was the meal of their dreams. I leaped sideways half a mile in one bound and their momentum carried them straight on by, but as I whirled to faced them another big black object shot past me from behind like a bat out of hell and I jumped again, just at random. Laughter came from two directions, and from a third Bess Huddleston's voice:

"They weren't after you, Mr. Goldwin, they smelled Mister coming and they're afraid of him. He teases them."

The bears were not in sight. The orangutan jumped up on the swing and off again. I said savagely, "My name is Goolenwangel."

Dr. Brady was shaking my hand. He said with a laugh, "Don't mind her, Mr. Goodwin. It's a pose. She pretends she can't remember the name of anyone not in the Social Register. Since her entire career is founded on snobbery—"

"Snob yourself," Bess Huddleston snorted. "You were born to it and believe in it. With me it's business. But for heaven's sake let's not—Mister, you devil, don't you dare tickle my feet!"

Mister went right ahead. He already had the red slippers off, and, depositing them right side up on a flagstone, he proceeded to tickle the sole of her right foot. She screamed and kicked him. He tickled the other foot, and she screamed again and kicked him with that. That appeared to satisfy him, for he started off, but his next performance was unpremeditated. A man in a butler's jacket, approaching with a tray of glasses and bottles, had just reached the end of the swing when Mister bumped him, and bumped him good. The man yelled and lost control, and down went the works. Dr. Brady caught one bottle on the fly, and I caught another, but everything else was shattered on the stones. Mister went twenty feet through the air and landed in a chair and sat there and giggled, and the man was trembling all over.

"For God's sake, Haskell," Bess Huddleston said, "don't leave now, with guests coming for dinner. Go to your room and have a drink and lie down. We'll clean this up."

"My name is Hoskins," the man said in a hollow tone.

"So it is. Of course it is. Go and have a drink."

The man went, and the rest of us got busy. When Mister got the idea, which was at once, he waddled over to help, and I'll say this much for him, he was the fastest picker-up of pieces of broken glass I have ever seen. Janet went and came back with implements, among them a couple of brooms, but the trouble was that you couldn't make a comprehensive sweep of it on account of the strips of turf between the flagstones. Larry went for another outfit of drinks, and finally Maryella solved the problem of the bits of glass in the grass strips by bringing a vacuum cleaner. Bess Huddleston stayed on the swing. Dr. Brady carried off the debris, and eventually we got back to normal, everybody with a drink, including Mister, only his was non-alcoholic, or I wouldn't have stayed. What that bird would have done with a couple of Martinis under his fur would have been something to watch from an airplane.

"This seems to be a day for breaking things," Bess Huddleston said, sipping an old-fashioned. "Someone broke my bottle of bath salts and it splattered all over the bathroom and just left it that way."

"Mister?" Maryella asked.

"I don't think so. He never goes in there. I didn't dare ask the servants."

But apparently at the Huddleston place there was no such thing as settling down for a social quarter of an hour, whether Mister was drunk or sober, only the next disturbance wasn't his fault, except indirectly. The social atmosphere was nothing to brag about anyhow, because it struck me that certain primitive feelings were being felt and not concealed with any great success. I'm not so hot at nuances, but it didn't take a Nero Wolfe to see that Maryella was working on Larry Huddleston, that the sight of the performance was giving Dr. Brady the fidgets in his facial muscles, that Janet was embarrassed and trying to pretend she didn't notice what was going on, and that Daniel was absent-mindedly drinking too much because he was worrying about something. Bess Huddleston had her ear cocked to hear what I was saying to Dr. Brady, but I was merely dating him to call at the office. He couldn't make it that evening, but tomorrow perhaps . . . his schedule was very crowded. . . .

The disturbance came when Bess Huddleston said she guessed she had better go and see if there was going to be any dinner or anyone to serve it, and sat up and put on her slippers. That is, she put one on; the second one, she stuck her foot in, let out a squeak, and jerked the foot out again.

"Damn!" she said. "A piece of glass in my slipper! Cut my toe!"

Mister bounced over to her, and the rest of us gathered around. Since Brady was a doctor, he took charge of matters. I didn't amount to much, a shallow gash half an inch long on the bottom of her big toe, but it bled some, and Mister started whining and wouldn't stop. Brother Daniel brought first-aid materials from the living room, and after Brady had applied a good dose of iodine, he did a neat job with gauze and tape.

"It's all right, Mister," Bess Huddleston said reassuringly. "You don't—hey!"

Mister had swiped the iodine bottle, uncorked it, and was carefully depositing the contents, drop by drop, onto one of the strips of turf. He wouldn't surrender it to Brady or Maryella, but he gave it to his mistress on demand, after re-corking it himself, and she handed it to her brother.

It was after six o'clock, and I wasn't invited to dinner, and anyway I had had enough zoology for one day, so I said good-bye and took myself off. When I got the roadster onto the highway and was among my fellows again, I took a long deep breath of the good old mixture of gasoline and air and the usual odors.

When I got back to the office Wolfe, who was making marks on a big map of Russia he had bought recently, said he would take my report later, so, after comparing the type on my sample with that on the Horrocks letter and finding they were written on the same machine, I went up to my room for a shower and a change. After dinner, back in the office, he told me to make it a complete recital, leaving out nothing, which meant that he had made no start and formed no opinion. I told him I preferred a written report, because when I delivered it verbally he threw me off the track by making faces and irritating me, but he leaned back and shut his eyes and told me to proceed.

It was nearly midnight when I finished, what with the usual interruptions. When he's doing a complete coverage, he thinks nothing of asking such a question as, "Did the animal pour the iodine on the grass with its right paw or its left?" If he were a movable object and went places himself it would save me a lot of breath, but then that's what I get paid for. Partly.

He stood up and stretched, and I yawned. "Well," I asked offensively, "got it sewed up? Including proof?"

"I'm sleepy," he said, starting off. At the door he turned. "You made the usual quantity of mistakes, naturally, but probably the only one of importance was your failure to investigate the matter of the broken bottle in Miss Huddleston's bathroom."

"Pah," I said. "If that's the best you can do. It was not a bottle of anonymous letters. Bath salts."

"All the same it's preposterous. It's even improbable. Break a bottle and simply go off, leaving it scattered around? No one would do that."

"You don't know that orangutan. I do."

"Not orangutan. Chimpanzee. It might have done it, yes. That's why you should have investigated. If the animal did not do it, there's something fishy about it. Highly unnatural. If Dr. Brady arrives by eight fifty-nine, I'll see him before I go up to the plant rooms. Good night."

Chapter 4

That was Tuesday night, August 19th. On Friday the 22nd Bess Huddleston got tetanus. On Monday the 25th she died. To show how everything from war to picnics depends on the weather, as Wolfe remarked when he was discussing the case with a friend the other day, if there had been a heavy rainfall in Riverdale between the 19th and 26th it would have been impossible to prove it was murder, let alone catch the murderer. Not that he showed any great—oh, well.

On Wednesday the 20th Dr. Brady came to the office for an interview with Wolfe, and the next day brother Daniel and nephew Larry came. About all we got out of that was that among the men nobody liked anybody. In the meantime, upon instructions from Wolfe, I was wrapping my tentacles about Janet, coaxing her into my deadly embrace. It really wasn't an unpleasant job, because Wednesday afternoon I took her to a ball game and was agreeably surprised to find that she knew a bunt from a base on balls, and Friday evening we went to the Flamingo Roof and I learned that she could dance nearly as well as Lily Rowan. She was no cuddler and a little stiff, but she went with the music and always knew what we were going to do. Saturday morning I reported to Wolfe regarding her as follows:

1. If she was toting a grievance against Bess Huddleston, it would take a smarter man than me to find out what it was.
2. There was nothing fundamentally wrong with her except that she would rather live in the country than the city.
3. She had no definite suspicion about who had sent the anonymous letters or anyone's motive for sending them.

Wolfe said, "Try Miss Timms for a change."

I didn't try to date Maryella for Saturday or Sunday, because Janet had told me they were all going to Saratoga for the weekend. Monday morning, I thought, was no time to start a romance, so I waited until afternoon to phone, got Maryella, and got the news. I went up to the plant rooms, where Wolfe was a sight to behold in his undershirt, cutting the tops from a row of vandas for propagation, and told him:

"Bess Huddleston is dead."

"Let me alone," he said peevishly. "I'm doing all I can. Someone will probably get another letter before long, and when—"

"No, sir. No more letters. I am stating facts. Friday evening tetanus set in from that cut on her toe, and about an hour ago she died. Maryella's voice was choked with emotion as she told me."

Wolfe scowled at me. "Tetanus?"

"Yes, sir."

"That would have been a five thousand dollar fee."

"It would have been if you had seen fit to do a little work instead of—"

"It was no good and you know it. I was waiting for another letter. File it away, including the letter to Mrs. Horrocks, to be delivered to her on request. I'm glad to be rid of it."

I wasn't. Down in the office, as I checked over the folder, consisting of the Horrocks letter, the snapshot of Janet, a couple of reports I had made and some memos Wolfe had dictated, I felt as if I was leaving a ball game in the fourth inning with the score a tie. But it looked as if nothing could be done about it, and certainly there was no use trying to badger Wolfe. I phoned Janet to ask if there was anything I could do, and she told me in a weak tired voice that as far as she knew there wasn't.

According to the obit in the *Times* the next morning, the funeral service was to be Wednesday afternoon, at the Belford Memorial Chapel on 73rd Street, and of course there would be a big crowd, even in August, for Bess Huddleston's last party. Cordially invited to meet death. I decided to go. Not merely, if I know myself, for curiosity or another look at Janet. It is not my custom to frequent memorial chapels to look at girls even if they're good dancers. Call it a hunch. Not that I saw anything criminal, only something incredible. I filed past the casket with the throng because from a distance I had seen it and couldn't believe it. But when I got close there it was. Eight black orchids that could have come from nowhere else in the world, and a card with his initials the way he scribbled them, "N.W."

When I got home, and Wolfe came down from the plant rooms at six o'clock, I didn't mention it. I decided it wasn't advisable. I needed to devote some thought to it.

It was that evening, Wednesday evening after the funeral, that I answered the doorbell, and who should I see on the stoop but my old colleague Inspector Cramer of the Homicide Squad. I hailed him with false enthusiasm and ushered him into the office, where Wolfe was making more marks on the map of Russia. They exchanged greetings, and Cramer sat in the red leather chair, took out a handkerchief and wiped perspiration from his exposed surfaces, put a cigar between his lips and sank his teeth in it.

"Your hair's turning gray," I observed. "You look as if you weren't getting enough exercise. A brain-worker like you—"

"God knows why you keep him," he said to Wolfe.

Wolfe grunted. "He saved my life once."

"Once!" I exclaimed indignantly. "Beginning—"

"Shut up, Archie. What can I do for you, Inspector?"

"You can tell me what you were doing for Bess Huddleston."

"Indeed." Wolfe's brows went up a shade. "You? The Homicide Bureau? Why do you want to know?"

"Because a guy is making himself a pest down at Headquarters. Her brother. He says she was murdered."

"He does?"

"Yes."

"Offering what evidence?"

"None at all."

"Then why bother me about it? Or yourself either?"

"Because we can't shut him up. He's even been to the Commissioner. And though he has no evidence, he has an argument. I'd like to tell you his argument."

Wolfe leaned back and sighed. "Go ahead."

"Well. He started on us last Saturday, four days ago. She got tetanus the day before. I don't need to tell you about that cut on her toe, since Goodwin was there—"

"I've heard about it."

"I'll bet you have. The brother, Daniel, said she

couldn't have got tetanus from that cut. He said it was a clean piece of glass that dropped into her slipper when the tray of glasses fell on the terrace. He saw it. And the slipper was a clean house slipper, nearly new and clean. And she hadn't been walking around barefooted. He claimed there couldn't possibly have been any tetanus germs in that cut, at least not enough to cause so violent an attack so soon. I sent a man up there Saturday night, but the doctor wouldn't let him see her, and of course he had no evidence—"

"Dr. Brady?"

"Yes. But the brother kept after us, especially when she died, and yesterday morning I sent a couple of men up to rub it off. I want to ask you, Goodwin, what was the piece of glass like? The piece in her slipper that cut her?"

"I knew you really came to see me," I told him genially. "It was a piece from one of the thick blue glasses that they had for old-fashioneds. Several of them broke."

Cramer nodded. "So they all say. We sent the slippers to the laboratory, and they say no tetanus germs. Of course there was another possibility, the iodine and the bandage. We sent all the stuff on that shelf to the laboratory, and the gauze was sterile, and it was good iodine, so naturally there were no germs in it. Under the circum—"

"Subsequent dressings," Wolfe muttered.

"No. The dressing Brady found on it when he was called up there Friday night was the one he had put on originally."

"Listen," I put in, "I know. By God. That orangutan. He tickled her feet. He rubbed germs on her—"

Cramer shook his head. "We went into that too. One of them suggested it—the nephew. That seems to be a possibility. It sounds farfetched to me, but of course it's possible. Now what the doctor says. Brady."

"Excuse me," Wolfe said. "You talked to those people.

Had Miss Huddleston nothing to say to them before she died? Any of them?"

"Not much. Do you know what tetanus does?"

"Vaguely."

"It does plenty. Like strychnine, only worse because there are no periods of relaxation and it lasts longer. When Brady got there Friday night her jaw was already locked tight. He gave her avertin to relieve her, and kept it up till the end. When my man was there Saturday night she was bent double backwards. Sunday she told Brady through her teeth she wanted to tell people good-bye, and he took them in one at a time. I've got their statements. Nothing significant, what you'd expect. Of course she only said a few words to each one—she was in bad shape. Her brother tried to tell her that her approaching death wasn't an accident, it was murder, but Brady and the nurse wouldn't let him."

"She herself had no such suspicion?"

"Not in evidence. You realize what she was like." Cramer shifted the cigar to the other side of his mouth. "What Brady says about the tetanus, one three-hundredth of a grain of the toxin is fatal. The bacilli and spores are more or less around everywhere, but of course especially in the neighborhood of horses. The soil around a barnyard reeks with it. I asked Brady what about his infecting the cut or the bandage with his own fingers when he dressed it, since he had just been riding, but he said he had washed his hands, and so had the Nichols girl, and she corroborated it. He said it was highly unlikely that there should have been tetanus bacilli on the piece of glass or her slipper or the skin of her toe or that animal's paw, at least enough of them to cause such a quick and virulent attack, but he said it was also unlikely that when a man walks across a street at a corner with a green light he should get run over, but sometimes he does. He says that he deeply regrets he didn't return Tuesday evening or

Wednesday and give her an injection of antitoxin, but he doesn't blame himself because no doctor alive would have done so. After the poison reached the nerve centers, as it had when Brady arrived Friday night, it was too late for antitoxin, though he tried it. Everything Brady said has been checked with the Examiner and is okay."

"I don't like his analogy," Wolfe declared. "A man crossing a street is extremely likely to get run over. That's why I never undertake it. However, that doesn't impeach Dr. Brady. I ask you again, Mr. Cramer, why do you bother me with all this, or yourself either?"

"That's what I came here to find out."

"Not the proper place. Try the inside of your head."

"Oh, that's all right," Cramer asserted. "I'm satisfied. It was accidental. But that damn brother won't let go. And before I get through with him and toss him out on his ear. I thought I'd better have a word with you. If there was anyone around there with murder in his heart, you ought to know. You would know. Since you had just started on a job for her. You're not interested in petty larceny. So I'd like to know what the job was."

"No doubt," Wolfe said. "Didn't any of those people tell you?"

"No."

"None of them?"

"No."

"Then how did you know she had hired me?"

"The brother told me about Goodwin being there, and that led me to question him. But he doesn't seem to know what your job was about."

"Neither do I."

Cramer took the cigar from his mouth and said vehemently, "Now look! How's it going to hurt you? Loosen up for once! I want to cross this off, that's all. I've got work to do! All I want to know—"

"Please!" Wolfe said curtly. "You say you are satisfied that the death was accidental. You have no shred of evidence of a crime. Miss Huddleston hired me for a confidential job. Her death does not release me, it merely deprives me of the job. If you had an action you could summon me, but you haven't. Will you have some beer?"

"No." Cramer glared. "My God, you can be honorable when you want to be! Will you answer a plain question? Do you think she was murdered?"

"No."

"Then you think it was purely accidental?"

"No."

"What the hell do you think?"

"Nothing at all. About that. I know nothing about it. I have no interest in it. The woman died, as all women do, may she rest in peace, and I lost a fee. Why don't you ask me this: if you knew what I know, if I told you all about the job she hired me for, would you feel that her death required further investigation?"

"Okay. I ask it."

"The answer is no. Since you have discovered no single suspicious circumstance. Will you have some beer?"

"Yes, I will," Cramer growled.

He consumed a bottle, got no further concessions either in information or in hypothetical questions, and departed.

I saw him to the door, returned to the office and remarked:

"Old Frizzle-top seems to be improving with age. Of course he has had the advantage of studying my methods. He seems to have covered the ground up there nearly as well as I could."

"Pfui." Wolfe pushed the tray aside to make room for the map. "Not that I don't agree with you. Nearly as well as you could, yes. But either he didn't have sense enough to learn everything that happened that afternoon, or he missed his best chance to expose a crime, if there was one. It hasn't rained the past week, has it? No."

I cocked an eye at him. "You don't say. How many guesses can I have?"

But he left it at that and got busy with the map, ignoring my questions. It was one of the many occasions when it would have been a pleasure to push him off of the Empire State Building, if there had been any way of enticing him there. Of course there was a chance that he was merely pulling my leg, but I doubted it. I know his tones of voice.

It ruined my night for me. Instead of going to sleep in thirty seconds it took me thirty minutes, trying to figure out what the devil he meant, and I woke up twice with nightmares, the first time because it was raining on me through the roof and each raindrop was a tetanus germ, and the second time I was lost in a desert where it hadn't rained for a hundred years. Next morning, after Wolfe had gone up to the plant rooms at nine o'clock, I got stubborn. I sat at my desk and went over that party at Riverdale in my mind, second by second, as I had reported it to Wolfe. And I got it. I would have hit it sooner if it hadn't been for various interruptions, phone calls and so on, but anyway finally there it was, as obvious as lipstick.

Provided one thing. To settle that I phoned Doc Vollmer, whose home and office were in a house down the street, and learned that tetanus, which carried death, had a third as many lives as a cat—one as a toxin, one as a bacillus, and one as a spore. The bacillus or the spore got in you and manufactured the toxin, which did the dirty work, traveling not with the blood but with the nerves. The bacillus and spore were both anaerobic, but could live in surface soil or dust for years and usually did, especially the spore.

And now what? Just forget it? Wolfe had, but then he wasn't human, whereas I was and am. Besides, it would be very neat if it got results, and it would teach Wolfe a lesson. It was nearly eleven o'clock, and I wanted to get out before he came downstairs, so I phoned up to him that I was leaving on an errand, and walked to the garage on Tenth Avenue and got the roadster. Heading uptown, I stopped at a hardware store near 42nd Street and went in and bought a long-bladed kitchen knife, a narrow garden trowel, and four paper bags. Then I went to a phone booth in a drug store at the corner and called the Huddleston number.

Maryella's voice answered, and I asked to speak to Miss Nichols. In a minute she was on, and I told her I was thinking she might be leaving there soon and I'd like to have her address.

"It's nice of you to call," she said. "It's a—pleasant surprise. Naturally I thought you—last week, I mean—I thought you were just being a detective."

"Don't kid me," I told her. "Anyone that dances the way you do being surprised at a phone call. Not that I suppose you're doing any dancing at present."

"Not now. No."

"Will you be leaving there soon?"

"Not this week. We're trying to help Mr. Huddleston straighten things up."

"Will you send me your address when you go?"

"Why—yes. Certainly. If you want it."

"I do you know. How would it be if I drove up there? Just to say hello?"

"When? Now?"

"Right now. I can be there in twenty minutes. I'd kind of like to see you."

"Why—" Silence. "That would be all right. If you want to take the trouble."

I told her it would be no trouble at all, hung up, went out to the roadster, and made for the entrance to the West Side Highway at 46th Street.

I admit my timing was terrible. If I had arrived, say, between twelve thirty and one, they might have been in the house having lunch, and I could have said I had already eaten and waited for Janet on the terrace, which would have been a perfect opportunity. Of course as it turned out that would have made a monkey of me, so it was just as well that I dubbed it. As it was, leaving the car outside the fence, with the knife in one hip pocket and the trowel in the other, and the folded paper bags in the side pocket of my coat, I walked across the lawn to where Larry stood near the pool, glowering at it. When he heard me coming he transferred the glower to me.

"Hello," I said amiably. "What, no alligators?"

"No. They're gone."

"And Mister? And the bears?"

"Yes. What the hell are you doing here?"

I suppose it would have been sensible to appease him, but he was really quite irritating. Tone and look both. So I said, "I came to play tag with Mister," and started for the house, but Janet appeared, cutting across the lawn. She looked prettier than I remembered her, or maybe not so much prettier as more interesting. Her hair was done differently or something. She said hello to me and let me have a hand to shake, and then told Larry:

"Maryella says you'll have to help her with those Corliss bills. Some of them go back before she came, and she doesn't seem to trust my memory."

Larry nodded at her, and, moving, was in front of me. "What do you want?" he demanded.

"Nothing special," I said. "Freedom of speech, freedom of religion, freedom—"

"If you've got a bill, mail it. You'll get about three per-cent."

I suppressed impulses and shook my head. "No bill. I came to see Miss Nichols."

"Yes you did. You came to snoop—"

But Janet had her hand on his arm. "Please, Larry. Mr. Goodwin phoned and asked to see me. Please?"

I would have preferred smacking him, and it was irritating to see her with her hand on his arm looking up at him the way she did, but when he turned and marched off towards the house I restrained myself and let him go.

I asked Janet, "What's eating him?"

"Well," she said, "after all, you are a detective. And his aunt has died—terrible, it was terrible—"

"Sure. If you want to call that grief. What was the crack about three per cent?"

"Oh . . ." She hesitated. "But there's nothing secret about it, goodness knows. Miss Huddleston's affairs are tangled up. Everybody thought she was rich, but apparently she spent it as fast as she made it."

"Faster, if the creditors are going to get three per-cent." I got started towards the terrace, and she came beside me. "In that case, the brother and the nephew are out of luck. I apologize to Larry. He's probably overcome by grief, after all."

"That's a mean thing to say," Janet protested.

"Then I take it back." I waved it away. "Let's talk about something else."

I was thinking the best plan was to sit with her on the terrace, with the idea of getting her to leave me alone there for a few minutes, which was all I needed, but the hot noon sun was coming straight down, and she went on into the house with me behind her. She invited me to sit on a couch with her, but with the tools in my hip pockets I thought it was safer to take a chair facing her. We had a conversation.

Of course the simplest thing would have been to tell her what I wanted to do and then go ahead and do it, and I deny that it was any suspicion of her, either as a letter writer or as a murderess, that kept me from doing that. It was the natural desire I had not to hurt her feelings by letting her know that my real purpose in coming was not just to see her. If things should develop it was good policy to have her friendly. So I played it for a solo. I was thinking it was about time to get on with it, and was figuring out an errand for her, preferably upstairs, that would be sure to keep her five minutes, when suddenly I saw something through the window that made me stare.

It was Daniel Huddleston on the terrace with a newspaper bundle under his arm and a long-bladed knife in one hand and a garden trowel in the other!

I stood up to see better.

"What is it?" Janet asked, and stood up too. I shushed her and whispered in her ear, "First lesson for a detective. Don't make any noise."

Brother Daniel stopped near the center of the terrace, in front of the swing, knelt down on a flagstone, deposited the newspaper bundle and some folded newspapers beside him, and the trowel, and plunged the knife into the strip of turf at the edge of the flagstone. There was nothing furtive about it; he didn't do any glancing over his shoulder, but he worked fast. With the trowel he scooped out a hunk of the turf, the width of the strip, about six inches long and three inches deep, and rolled it in a piece of newspaper. Then a second one, to the right of the first hole, and then a third one, to the left, wrapping each separately.

"What on earth does he think he's doing?" Janet whispered. I squeezed her arm.

He was about done. Opening the package he had

brought with him, he produced three strips of turf the size and shape of those he had just dug out, fitted them into the trench he had made, pressed them with his foot until they were level with the flagstone, remade the package with the three hunks he had removed, and the knife and trowel, and went off as if he were bound somewhere.

I took Janet's hand and gave her an earnest eye. "Listen, girlie," I said, "my one fault is curiosity. Otherwise I am perfect. Don't forget that. It's time for your lunch anyway."

She said something to my back as I made for the door. I emerged onto the terrace cautiously, slid across and into the hedge of shrubbery, made a hole and looked through. Daniel was forty paces away, going across the lawn not in the direction of the drive where my car was but the other way, off to the right. I decided to give him another twenty paces before emerging, and it was well that I did, for suddenly a voice sounded above me:

"Hey, Uncle Dan! Where you going?"

Daniel stopped in his tracks and whirled. I twisted my neck, and through the leaves got a glimpse of Larry's head sticking out of an upper window, and Maryella's beside it.

Larry shouted, "We need you!"

"See you later!" Daniel yelled.

"But it's time for lunch!" Maryella called.

"See you later!" Daniel turned and was off.

"Now that's a performance," Maryella said to Larry.

"Cuckoo," Larry declared.

Their heads went in. But they might still have been looking out, so I scooted along the side of the house to the corner, and from there circled wide around evergreens and similar obstructions before swinging into the direction Daniel had taken. He wasn't in sight. This part of the premises was new to me, and the first thing I knew I ran smack into the fence in the middle of a thicket. I couldn't fight my way through on account of noise, so I doubled around, dashed along the edge of the thicket, and pretty soon hit a path. No sight of Daniel. The path took me to a series of stone steps up a steep bank, and up I went. Getting to the top, I saw him. A hundred feet ahead was a gate in the fence, and he was shutting the gate and starting down a lane between rows of little trees. The package was under his arm. In a way I was more interested in the package than I was in him. What if he threw it down a sewer? So I closed up more than I would have for an ordinary tailing job, and proceeding through the gate, followed him down the lane. At the end of the lane, not far ahead, he stopped, and I dived into the trees.

He had stopped at a curb, a paved street. The way cars were rolling by, apparently it was a main traffic street; and that point was settled when a double-decker bus jerked to a stop right square in front of Daniel, and he climbed on and off the bus went.

I hotfooted it to the corner. It was Marble Avenue. Riverdale is like that. The bus was too far away to read its number, and no taxi was in sight in either direction. I stepped into the street, into the path of the first car coming, and held up a commanding palm. By bad luck it was occupied by the two women that Helen Hokinson used for models, but there was no time to pick and choose. I hopped into the back seat, gave the driver a fleeting glimpse of my detective license, and said briskly:

"Police business. Step on it and catch up with a bus that's ahead."

The one driving emitted a baby scream. The other one said, "You don't look like a policeman. You get out. If you don't we'll drive to a police station."

"Suit yourself, madam. While we sit and talk the most dangerous gangster in New York is escaping. He's on the bus."

"Oh! He'll shoot at us."

"No. He isn't armed."

"Then why is he dangerous?"

"For God's sake," I reached for the door latch, "I'll take a car with a man in it!"

But the car started forward. "You will not," the driver said fiercely. "I'm as good a driver as any man. My husband says so."

She was okay at that. Within a block she had it up to fifty, and she was good at passing, and it wasn't long before we caught up with the bus. At least, a bus. When it stopped at a corner I told her to get alongside, which she did neatly, and with my hand over my face I looked for him and there he was.

"I'm shadowing him," I told the ladies. "I think he's on his way to meet a crooked politician. The first empty taxi we see you can let me out if you want to, but of course he might suspect a taxi, whereas he never would suspect a car like this with two good-looking well-dressed women in it."

The driver looked grim. "In that case," she declared, "it is our duty."

And by gum she crawled along behind that bus for a good three-quarters of an hour, to Riverside Drive, the whole length of the Drive, over to Broadway, and on downtown. I thought the least I could do was furnish diversion, which I did with tales of my experiences with gangsters and kidnappers and so forth. When Daniel was still on the bus after crossing 42nd Street I decided in disgust that he was probably bound for Headquarters, and I was so deeply considering the feasibility of intercepting him before he got there that I nearly missed it when he hopped to the sidewalk at 34th Street. Paying the ladies with thanks and a cordial smile, I jumped out and dodged through the midday shopping mob, and almost lost him. I picked him up going west on 34th.

At Eighth Avenue he turned uptown. I kept twenty yards behind.

At 35th he turned west again.

That was when I got suspicious. Naturally. On he went, straight as a bullet. When he kept on west of Ninth Avenue, there was no question about it. I closed up. He began looking at the numbers on buildings, and came to the stoop and started up. Boy, I'm telling you, they don't get away from me. I get my man. I had trailed this one the length of New York, hanging on like a bulldog, right to Nero Wolfe's door.

Chapter 5

I had been thinking fast the last two blocks. I had considered, and rejected, three different maneuvers to keep Wolfe from finding out. They all seemed good, but I knew damn well none of them was good enough. He would find out all right, no matter what I did. So I bounded up the steps past Daniel, greeted him, let us in with my key, and took him to the office.

Wolfe, at his desk, frowned at us. "How do you do, Mr. Huddleston. Archie. Where have you been?"

"I know," I said, "it's about lunch time, so I'll make it brief. First cast a glance at this." I took the knife, the trowel, and the paper bags from my pockets and put them on his desk.

Daniel stared and muttered something.

"What is this flummery?" Wolfe demanded.

"No flummery," I asserted. "Tools. It still didn't rain last night. So I went to Riverdale to get the piece of turf where the orangutan poured the iodine. Brother Daniel had the same idea. He was just ahead of me. He's got it in that newspaper. I thought he might be going to toss it in the river, so I tailed him and he led me here. So I look foolish but not dumb. Now you can laugh."

He didn't. He looked at Daniel. "Is that what you have in that package, Mr. Huddleston?"

"It is," Daniel said. "I want—"

"Why did you bring it to me? I'm not a chemist. You are."

"Because I want to authenticate it. I want—"

"Take it to the police."

"No." Daniel looked and sounded determined. "They think I'm nothing but a nuisance. Maybe I am. But if I analyze this myself, without someone to—"

"Don't analyze it yourself. You have colleagues, friends, haven't you?"

"None I would want to give this to."

"Are you sure you have the piece where the iodine was poured?"

"I am. A few drops were on the edge of the flagstone. I also have pieces taken from each side of that piece, for comparison."

"Naturally. Who suggested this step to you?"

"No one. It occurred to me this morning, and I immediately went up there—"

"Indeed. I congratulate you. Take it to the Fisher Laboratories. You know them, don't you?"

"Certainly." Daniel flushed. "I happen not to have any cash at the moment. They are expensive."

"Establish credit. Your sister's estate. Aren't you her nearest relative?"

"There is no estate. The liabilities greatly exceed the assets."

Wolfe looked annoyed. "You are careless not to have cash. Confound it, you should have cash. You understand, sir, my finger is not in this pie. I am not concerned. My lunch is ready. I should bid you good day. But you seem to be capable of using your brains, and that is so rare a phenomenon it is a pity to waste it. Archie, phone

Mr. Weinbach at the Fisher Laboratories. Tell him to expect Mr. Huddleston, to rush the analysis he requires, and to charge it to me. You can pay the bill, sir, at your convenience."

Daniel hesitated. "I have a habit—I am extremely backward about paying bills—"

"You'll pay this one. I'll see that you do. What is argyrol?"

"Argyrol? Why—it's a silver-protein compound. Silver vietllin."

"It stains like iodine. Could tetanus bacilli live in it?"

Daniel considered. "I believe they could. It's far weaker—"

Wolfe nodded impatiently. "Tell Mr. Weinbach to try for it." He got up. "My lunch is waiting."

After I had finished the phone call and ushered Daniel out, with his package, I joined Wolfe in the dining room. Since no discussion of business was permitted at meals, I waited until we were back in the office again before observing:

"I ought to tell you that Janet saw him lifting that turf, and Maryella and the nephew—"

"There is no reason to tell me. I am not concerned." He pointed to the knife and trowel, still on his desk. "Where did you get those things?"

"Bought them."

"Please put them somewhere. They are not to appear on the expense account."

"Then I'll keep them in my room."

"Do so. By all means. Please take a letter to Mr. Hoehn."

His tone said, and that's the end of Miss Huddleston and her affairs for this office, for you, and for me.

No doubt it would have been, except for his vanity. Or perhaps it wasn't vanity; it may be that the reason he permitted his privacy to be invaded again by brother Daniel was that he wanted to impress on him the desirability of getting the bill of the Fisher Laboratories paid as soon as possible. At any rate, when Daniel turned up some hours later, a little before seven that evening, Fritz was told to bring him to the office. At first sight of him I knew he had something, by the look in his eye and the set of his jaw. He tramped over to Wolfe's desk and announced:

"My sister was murdered."

He got an envelope from his pocket, took out a paper and unfolded it, and fumbled the job because his hands were trembling. He swayed a little, steadied himself with a hand on the edge of the desk, looked around for a chair, and sat down.

"I guess I'm a little weak from excitement," he said apologetically. "Then I had only an apple for breakfast, and I haven't eaten anything since."

It was probably the one thing in the world he could have said to keep Wolfe from telling him to go to the police and telling me to bounce him out. The one kind of man that never gets the gate at that house is one with an empty stomach. Glaring at him, not sympathetically but indignantly, Wolfe pushed a button and, when Fritz appeared, inquired:

"How far along is the soup?"

"Quite ready, sir, except for the mushrooms."

"Bring a bowl of it, crackers, cottage cheese, and hot tea."

Daniel tried to protest, but Wolfe didn't even listen. He heaved a deep sigh and leaned back and shut his eyes, a man who had eaten nothing but an apple for twenty-four hours being too painful an object to look at. When Fritz came with the tray I had a table ready in front of Daniel, and he wolfed a couple of crackers and blew on a spoonful of soup and swallowed it.

I had acquired the sheet of paper he had taken from the envelope, a report sheet from Fisher Laboratories, and was looking it over. After some more spoonfuls Daniel said:

"I knew it. I was sure of it. There couldn't—"

"Eat!" Wolfe commanded sternly.

"I'm eating. I'm all right. You were correct about the argyrol. That was a good guess. Argyrol and nothing else." A fork conveyed a hunk of cottage cheese to Daniel's mouth, but he went on, "Not a trace of iodine. And millions of tetanus bacilli, hundreds of millions. Weinbach said he never saw anything like it. And they were all concentrated on the one piece of turf, on the grass stems and the soil surface. The other two pieces had no sign either of the silver vietllin or the tetanus. Weinbach said . . ."

The doorbell rang, but I kept my seat and left it for Fritz because I had no reason to expect any undesirable intrusions. As it turned out, however, it was exactly the kind of invasion Wolfe resents more than anything else. An insurance salesman or a wife wanting her husband tailed is merely a mosquito to be brushed off, with me to do the brushing, but this wasn't as simple as that. The sound of Fritz's voice came from the hall, in indignant protest, and then the door flew open and Inspector Cramer strode in. I mean strode. His first glance caught me, and was it withering. Then he saw who Daniel was, emitted a triumphal grunt, spread his feet apart, and rasped out:

"Come along, you!" And to me: "You too, bud! Come on!"

I grinned at him. "If you ever find time to glance over an interesting document called the Constitution of the United—"

"Shut up, Archie," Wolfe snapped. "Mr. Cramer. What in the name of heaven is the matter with you?"

"Not a thing," Cramer said sarcastically. "Matter with

me? Not a damn thing." I never saw him sorer or sourer. "Listen!" he said. He stepped to the desk and tapped a heavy finger on it, sounding like a hammer. "Last night, sitting right at this desk, what did you say? What did you tell me?"

Wolfe was grimacing with distaste. "Your tone and manner, Mr. Cramer—"

"You said, in case you've forgotten, that you weren't interested in the death of Bess Huddleston! Knew nothing about it! Weren't interested!" Cramer went on tapping the desk. "Well, this afternoon somebody in my office got an idea—we do that once in a while! I sent a man up there, and young Huddleston showed him where the monkey poured some of that iodine, and when he went to take some of that turf for analysis, he found it had already been taken! It had been carefully filled up with other turf, but the grass didn't match. He asked questions, and he learned that Daniel Huddleston had done it, taken the turf away, and Goodwin had been there and gone with him!"

"Not with him," I corrected emphatically. "After him."

Cramer ignored me. "We went for Huddleston and couldn't find him. So I come to see you. You and Goodwin. And what do I find? By God! I find Huddleston! Sitting here eating! This is the rawest one you've ever pulled! Removing evidence, destroying evidence—"

"Nonsense," Wolfe said curtly and coldly. "Stop shouting. If you wish to know the purpose of Mr. Huddleston's visit—"

"Not from you I don't! I'll get it from him! And from Goodwin! And separately! I'm taking them downtown."

"No," Wolfe said. "Not from my office."

That was the central point of the situation. Twenty minutes earlier Daniel's empty stomach was all that had kept Wolfe from chasing him to the police, and it wouldn't have hurt his appetite any if I had gone along to keep

Daniel company, but this was different. For a cop to remove persons from the house, any person whatever, with or without a charge or a warrant, except at Wolfe's instigation, was an intolerable insult to his pride, his vanity, and his sense of the fitness of things. So as was to be expected, he acted with a burst of energy amounting to violence. He sat up straight in his chair.

"Mr. Cramer," he said, "sit down."

"Not a chance." Cramer meant it. "You're not going to take me in with one of your goddamn—"

"Archie, show Mr. Cramer that report from the Fisher Laboratories."

I stuck it under his nose. His impulse was to push it away, but no cop, not even an Inspector, dares to refuse to look at a paper. So he snatched it and scowled at it. Daniel started to say something, but Wolfe shushed him, and Daniel finished off the cheese and the last cracker, and put sugar in his tea and began to stir it.

"So what?" Cramer growled. "How do I know—"

"I sometimes doubt if you know anything," Wolfe said shortly. "I was not and am not interested in Miss Huddleston's death, though you and Mr. Huddleston and Archie keep pestering me about it. I have no client. My client died. You are even affronted to find Mr. Huddleston here eating. If he's hungry, why the devil shouldn't he eat? When he appeared here at one o'clock with that turf, I told him to take it to the police. He said they regarded him as a nuisance. Why he returned here with the laboratory report, I do not know; I only know he was hungry. If you are disgruntled because you have no assurance that the piece of turf examined by the laboratory is the piece onto which the chimpanzee poured some of the contents of the bottle of supposed iodine, I can't help it. Why didn't you get the turf yourself when Mr. Huddleston first called on you, five days ago? It was an obvious thing to do."

"I didn't know then that the chimpanzee had poured—"

"You should have. Proper questioning would have got it. Either it was worth investigating competently, or not at all. Well, sir, there's your report. Keep it. You'll get a bill for it from the Fisher Laboratories. Archie, make a note of that. It wasn't iodine in that bottle; it was argyrol, and it was reeking with tetanus bacilli. An uncommonly ugly thing to do. I have never heard of a more objectionable way of committing murder, nor of an easier or simpler one. I trust, sir, that you'll make an arrest. You should, since you have only five people to deal with—the five who were there, not counting Archie—"

"Wait a minute," Daniel protested. "You're wrong. That bottle could have been put there any time—"

Wolfe shook his head. "No. Only that afternoon. If we had to we could argue that it is not credible that it was left in the cupboard for an extended period, for just anyone to use, but we don't have to. The bottle in that cupboard contained good iodine at four o'clock that afternoon."

Cramer growled. Daniel demanded, "How do you know that?"

"Because it was used at that hour. By Archie. He tripped on an alligator and scratched his hand."

"By God," Cramer said, and sat down. Daniel looked at me, and I nodded at him.

Daniel looked at Wolfe, his jaw hanging open and his face gray. "Then it c-couldn't have been—" he stammered.

"Couldn't have been what?" Cramer demanded.

"It couldn't have been someone—" Daniel shook his head weakly, as if trying to reject something. Suddenly he exclaimed fiercely, "I can't believe that! One of them? Those two girls or Larry or Brady?"

"Or you, sir," Wolfe said dryly. "You were there. As for your trying to get the police started on it, you may be more devious than you look. Save your indignation. Calm yourself. Your digestive processes will make a botch of that soup and cheese if you don't. So, Mr. Cramer, I give you that. It was an impromptu job. Not that it was unpremeditated; far from it; it was carefully prepared; an iodine bottle had been emptied and washed and replenished with argyrol and an army of tetanus germs."

Wolfe compressed his lips. "Very ugly. It would take an extremely unattractive person to think of that, let alone do it. It was done. I presume a situation was to be created requiring the use of the iodine; in fact, there is reason to believe that it had been created, or was in process; but the accident on the terrace provided an opportunity too good to be missed. From the standpoint of technique, it was brilliantly conceived and managed. Only two things needed to be done: drop a piece of glass into Miss Huddleston's slipper, which was quite simple with everyone jostling around picking up the pieces, and substitute the bottle of bogus iodine for the one that was in the cupboard. With no risk whatever. If Miss Huddleston shook the glass out of her slipper before putting it on, if for any reason she didn't cut herself, the bottle could be switched again and nothing lost. There is a point, of course: if the bottle in the cupboard had a different kind of label—"

"They all had the same label," Cramer rumbled.

"All?"

"Yes. There were seven bottles of iodine in that house, counting the kitchen, and they were all the same, size and shape and label."

"They bought it wholesale," I explained, "on account of Mister and the bears."

"That," Wolfe said, "is precisely the sort of thing you would know, Mr. Cramer. Seven. Not eight. Seven. And of course you had it all analyzed and it was all good iodine."

"It was. And what the hell is there in that to be sarcastic about? It clears up your point, don't it? And I might mention another point. The murderer had to leave the terrace, go in the house, between the time the glasses got broken and the time Miss Huddleston cut herself, to switch the iodine bottles."

Wolfe shook his head. "That offers nothing. They all went in the house during that period. Miss Nichols went for brooms and pans. The nephew went for another tray of supplies. Miss Timms went for a vacuum cleaner. Dr. Brady carried off the debris."

Cramer stared at him in exasperation. "And you know nothing about it! Jesus. You're not interested!"

"I didn't," Daniel put in. "I didn't leave the terrace during that period."

"So far as I know," Wolfe agreed, "that is correct. But if I were you I wouldn't brag about it. You went for the iodine. It was the bottle you handed to Dr. Brady that he used. Your jaw is loose again. You bounce, Mr. Huddleston, from wrath to indignation, with amazing agility. Frankly, I doubt if it is possible to suspect you of murdering your sister. If you did it, your facial dexterity surpasses anything in my experience. If you'll stay and dine with me, I'll reach a decision on that before the meal is finished. Partridges in marinade. *En escabeche.*" His eyes gleamed. "They are ready for us." He pushed back his chair and got himself onto his feet. "So, Mr. Cramer, it seems likely that it is limited to four, which simplifies your task. You'll excuse me, I'm sure—"

"Yeah," Cramer said, "glad to." He was up too. "But you'll enjoy your partridges alone. Huddleston and Goodwin are going with me." His glance took us in. "Let's go."

Wolfe looked displeased. "I have already cleared away the brush for you. If you insist on seeing them this evening, they can call at your office—say at ten o'clock?"

"No. They're coming now."

Wolfe's chin went up. His mouth opened and then closed again. It was an interesting sight, especially for me, knowing as I do how hard he is to flabbergast, next to impossible, but I can't truthfully say I enjoyed it, because of who was doing it. So I spoke up:

"I'm staying for the partridges. And I may or may not show up at ten o'clock, depending—"

"To hell with you," Cramer rumbled. "I'll deal with you later. We'll go, Mr. Huddleston."

Wolfe took a step, and his voice was as close to trembling with rage as it ever got. "Mr. Huddleston is my invited guest!"

"I've uninvited him. Come, Mr. Huddleston."

Wolfe turned to Daniel. He was controlling himself under insufferable provocation. "Mr. Huddleston. I have invited you to my table. You are under no compulsion, legal or moral, to accompany this man on demand. He struts and blusters. Later Mr. Goodwin will drive you—"

But Daniel said firmly, "I guess I'll go along with him, Mr. Wolfe. After the days I've spent trying to get them started on this . . ."

The partridge was swell, and I ate nearly as much as Wolfe did. Otherwise it was one of the dullest meals I had ever had under Wolfe's roof. He didn't say a word, clear to the coffee.

Chapter 6

I described that scene in detail, because if it hadn't been for that I doubt if the murderer of Bess Huddleston would ever have been caught. One of Cramer's bunch might possibly have doped it out, but they never in the world would have got enough evidence for an arrest. And Wolfe, with no client and no commitment, was through with it, or would have been if Cramer hadn't kidnapped a dinner guest right under his nose and made him so damn mad he had to take Amphojel twice that evening.

Twice. The first dose was right after dinner, when he sent me up to his room for the bottle. The second was long after midnight, when I got home after my call on Inspector Cramer downtown. I sneaked quietly up the two flights to my room, but was just starting to undress when the house phone on my table buzzed, and, answering it and getting a summons, I descended to Wolfe's room and entered. The light was on and he wasn't in his bed, and, proceeding to his bathroom, I found him taking another shot of Amphojel, with a scowl on his face that would have scared Joe Louis right out of the ring. He was a spectacle anyway, draped in the ten yards of yellow silk that it took to make him a suit of pajamas.

"Well?" he demanded.

"Nothing. Routine. Questions and a signed statement."

"He'll pay for this." Wolfe made a face like an infuriated gargoyle and put the Amphojel bottle back in the cabinet. "I haven't had to take this stuff since that hideous experiment with eels in the spring. He'll pay for it. Go to Riverdale early in the morning. Consult the stableman and learn—"

"I doubt if there is one. The horses are gone. The creditors get two percent."

"Find him. Wherever he is. I wish to know whether anyone has recently removed anything, any material, from the vicinity of the stable. A small paper bag filled at the manure pile would have been ideal. Question him. If he's difficult, bring him here. Also—is there a servant on the place?"

I nodded. "The butler. I think he's hanging on hoping to get paid."

"Ask him about that bottle that Miss Huddleston found broken in her bathroom. Whatever he knows about it. Ask any other servant who was there at the time. All details possible—"

"The others too? Maryella, Janet, Larry—"

"No. Mention it to no one but the servants. Phone before returning. Before you go, leave phone numbers on my desk—Riverdale, Mr. Huddleston, Dr. Brady—that's all. He'll pay for this. Good night."

So we had a case. We had no client, no retainer, and no fee in sight, but at least we had a case, which was better than sitting around on my tail listening to the radio.

I made six hours' sleep do me, and before eight o'clock next morning I was up at Riverdale. I didn't phone in advance, since I had to go anyway to get my car which I had left on the driveway the day before. Greeted at the door by Hoskins, I was told that the stableman was gone and maybe Maryella had his address. I would have preferred asking Janet or even Larry, but Hoskins said they were both late sleepers and Maryella was already eating breakfast, so I got the address from her, and by good luck it wasn't Bucyrus, Ohio, but merely Brooklyn. Whatever else you want to say about Brooklyn, and so do I, it does have one big advantage, it's close.

That errand was one of the simplest I have ever performed, once I found the address and the stableman. His name was Tim Lavery and a scar on his cheek made him look mean until he grinned. I started with him cautiously, pretending that my mind was on something else, but soon saw that it wasn't necessary to sneak up on him, and put it to him straight.

"Sure," he said, "one day about a month ago, maybe a little more, Doc Brady filled up a box he brought, an empty candy box. I helped him. He said he wanted it for a test. One of his patients had died of tetanus—I forget her name—"

I pretended there was nothing to be excited about. "Where'd he take it from? The stall?"

"No. The pile. I dug into the middle of the pile for him."

"Who was with him that day? One of the girls?"

Tim shook his head. "He was alone when he did that. They had been riding—I forget who was with him that day—and they went to the house and then he came back alone with that box and said what he wanted."

"Do you remember the day? The date?"

The best he could do on that was the last week in July. I got the details all filled in, made sure that he would be available if and when needed, and, leaving, stopped at the first phone booth and called Wolfe. Answering from the plant rooms and therefore with his mind occupied, he displayed no exultation, which he wouldn't anyway, and informed me that my discovery made no change in the rest of my assignment.

Arriving at the Huddleston place in Riverdale a little

after ten o'clock, my luck still held. Instead of stopping by the side gate, I continued along the drive, where another gate opened onto a path leading to the back door, and Hoskins was there in the kitchen having a conversation with a depressed-looking female in a maid's uniform. They acted reserved but not hostile; in fact, Hoskins invited me to have a cup of coffee, which I accepted. Taking an inventory as a precaution against any unwelcome interruptions, I was told that Larry and Maryella had both gone out, Daniel hadn't shown up that morning, no city employees were on the premises, and Janet had just had breakfast in bed. The field was clear, but I had a hunch that a delegation from Cramer's office might be appearing any minute, so I got down to business without wasting any time.

They both remembered all about it. Shortly after lunch that Tuesday afternoon Hoskins had been summoned to Miss Huddleston's room upstairs and requested to take a look at the bathroom. Broken glass was everywhere, in the tub, on the floor, the remnants of a large bottle of bath salts that had been kept on a high shelf above the bathtub. Miss Huddleston hadn't done it. Hoskins hadn't done it. The maid, summoned, said she hadn't done it, and then she and Hoskins cleaned up the mess. I asked what about the orangutan. Possibly, they said, with that beast anything was possible, but it had not been permitted upstairs and seldom went there, and had not been observed inside the house that day.

I filled in details all I could, even asking to view the remains of the broken bottle, which they said had been thick and heavy and creamy yellow in color, but that had been carted away. Then I asked Hoskins to let me take a look at the bathroom, and when we started for the stairs the maid came along, mumbling something about Miss

Nichols' breakfast tray. Bess Huddleston's room was more like a museum than a bedroom, the walls covered with framed autographed photographs and letters, and all the available space filled with everything from a lady manikin in an Eskimo suit to a string of Chinese lanterns, but what I was interested in was the bathroom. It was all colors, the World War camouflage type, or Devil's Rainbow. It made me too dizzy to do a decent job of inspection, but I managed to note such details as the position of the shelf on which the bottle of bath salts had stood. There was a new bottle there, nearly full, and I was reaching for it to take it down to look at it when I suddenly jerked around and cocked an ear and stepped to the door. Hoskins was standing in the middle of the room in a state of suspended animation, his back to me.

"Who screamed?" I demanded.

"Down the hall," he said without turning. "There's nobody but Miss Nichols—"

There had been nothing ear-piercing about it, in fact I had barely heard it, and there were no encores, but a scream is a scream. I marched past Hoskins and through the door, which was standing open, to the hall, and kept going.

"Last door on the right," Hoskins said behind me. I knew that, having been in Janet's room before. The door was shut. I turned the knob and went in, and saw no one, but another door, standing open, revealed a corner of a bathroom. As I started for it the maid's voice came out:

"Who is it?"

"Archie Goodwin. What—"

The maid appeared in the doorway, looking flustered. "You can't come in! Miss Nichols isn't dressed!"

"Okay." I halted out of delicacy. "But I heard a scream. Do you need any rescuing, Janet?"

"Oh, no!" the undressed invisible Janet called, in a voice so weak I could just hear it. "No, I'm all right!" The voice was not only weak, it was shaky.

"What happened?" I asked.

"Nothing serious," the maid said. "A cut on her arm. She cut herself with a piece of glass."

"She what?" I goggled. But without waiting for an answer, I stepped across and walked through the maid into the bathroom. Janet, undressed in the fullest sense of the word and wet all over, was seated on a stool. Ignoring protests and shaking off the maid, who was as red as a beet having her modesty shocked by proxy, I got a towel from a rack and handed it to Janet.

"Here," I said, "this will protect civilization. How the dickens did you do that?"

I lifted her left arm for a look. The cut, nearly an inch long, halfway between the wrist and the elbow, looked worse than it probably was on account of the mixture of blood and iodine. It certainly didn't seem to be worth fainting for, but Janet's face looked as if she might be going to faint. I took the iodine bottle out of her hand and put the cork in it.

"I never scream," Janet said, holding the towel up to her chin. "Really, I never do. But it seemed so . . . cutting myself with glass . . . so soon after Miss Huddleston . . ." She swallowed. "I didn't scream when I cut myself; I'm not quite that silly, really I'm not. I screamed when I saw the piece of glass in the bath brush. It seemed so—"

"Here it is," the maid said.

I took it. It was a piece of jagged glass, creamy yellow, not much bigger than my thumbnail.

"It's like a piece of that bottle that was broke in Miss Huddleston's room that you was asking about," the maid said.

"I'll keep it for a souvenir," I announced, and dropped it into the pocket where I had put the iodine bottle, and picked up the bath brush from the floor. It was soaking wet. "You mean you got in the tub and got soaped, and started to use the brush and cut yourself, and looked at the brush and saw the piece of glass wedged in the bristles, and screamed. Huh?"

Janet nodded. "I know it was silly to scream—"

"I was in the room," the maid said, "and I ran in and—"

"Okay," I cut her off. "Get me some gauze and bandages."

"There in the cabinet," Janet said.

I did a neat job on her, using plenty of gauze because the cut was still trying to bleed. Where she needed the blood was in her face, which was still white and scared, though she tried to smile at me when she thanked me.

I patted her on a nice round shoulder. "Don't mention it, girlie. I'll wait downstairs until you get dressed. I like you in that towel, but I think it would be sensible to go to a doctor and get a shot of antitoxin. I'll drive you. When you—"

"Anitoxin?" she gasped.

"Sure." I patted her again. "Just a precaution. Nothing to worry about. I'll be waiting downstairs."

Hoskins, hovering around in the hall, was relieved when I told him there was nothing for him to do except to get me a piece of paper to wrap the bath brush in. I waited till I was alone, down in the living room, to take the iodine bottle from my pocket, uncork it, and smell it. Whatever it was, it wasn't iodine. I put the cork back in good and tight, went to a lavatory across the hall and washed my hands, and then found a telephone and dialed Wolfe's number.

He answered himself, from the plant rooms since it wasn't eleven o'clock yet, and I gave it to him, all of it. When I finished he said immediately and urgently:

"Get her away from there!"

"Yes, sir, that is my intention—"

"Confound it, at once! Why phone me? If Mr. Cramer goes—"

"Please," I said firmly. "She was naked. I have no white horse, and she hasn't got much hair, at least not that much. As soon as she's dressed we're off. I was going to suggest that you phone Doc Vollmer and tell him to have a dose of antitoxin ready. We'll be there in about half an hour. Or I can phone him from here—"

"No. I will. Leave as soon as possible."

"Righto."

I went upstairs to the door of Janet's room and called to her that I'd be waiting by the side gate, and then went out and turned the car around and took it that far back down the drive. I was debating what course to follow if a police car put in an appearance, when here she came down the path, a little wobbly on her pins and far from pert but her buttons all buttoned. I helped her in and tore out of there with the gravel flying.

She didn't seem to feel like talking. I explained to her about Doc Vollmer being an old friend of ours, with his home and office on the same block as Nero Wolfe's house, so I was taking her there, and I tried a few leading questions, such as whether she had any idea how the piece of glass got into the bristles of her bath brush, but she didn't seem to be having any ideas. What she needed was a strong man to hold her hand, but I was driving. She had simply had the daylights scared out of her.

I had no explaining to do at Doc Vollmer's, since Wolfe had talked to him on the phone, and we weren't in there more than twenty minutes altogether. He cleaned the cut thoroughly, applied some of his own iodine, gave her the antitoxin in that arm, and then took me to an inside room and asked me for the iodine bottle I had. When I gave it to him he uncorked it, smelled it, frowned, poured a little of the contents into a glass vial, corked it again even tighter than I had, and handed it back to me.

"She'll be all right," he said. "What a devilish trick! Tell Mr. Wolfe I'll phone him as soon as possible."

I escorted Janet back out to the car. It was only a

couple of hundred feet from there to Wolfe's door, and I discovered that I couldn't drive the last thirty of them because two cars were parked in front. Janet hadn't even asked why I was taking her to Wolfe's house. Apparently she was leaving it up to me. I gave her a reassuring grin as I opened the door with my key and waved her in.

Not knowing who the callers might be, the owners of the cars in front, instead of taking her straight to the office I ushered her into the front room. But one of them was there, sprawled in a chair, and when Janet saw him she emitted an exclamation. It was Larry Huddleston. I greeted him, invited Janet to sit, and not wanting to use the connecting door to the office, went around by the hall. Wolfe wasn't in the office, but two more visitors were, and they were Dr. Brady and Daniel Huddleston, evidently, judging from their attitudes, not being chummy.

Oho, I thought, we're having a party, and went to the kitchen, and there was Wolfe.

He was standing by the long table, watching Fritz rub a spice mixture into slices of calf's liver, and watching with him, standing beside him, closer to him than I had ever seen any woman or girl of any age tolerated, with her hand slipped between his arm and his bulk, was Maryella.

Wolfe gave me a fleeting glance. "Back, Archie? We're doing mock terrapin. Miss Timms had a suggestion." He leaned over to peer at the liver, straightened, and sighed clear to the bottom. He turned to me: "And Miss Nichols?"

"In front. Doc Vollmer took a sample and will phone as soon as possible."

"Good. On the coldest shelf, Fritz; the time is uncertain; and leave the door to Archie. Archie, we are busy and not available. All of us. Come, Miss Timms."

She couldn't cling to him as they went through the door, because there wasn't room.

Chapter 7

Dr. Brady said sharply, "I've been waiting here over half an hour. How long will this take? I'm due at my office at one o'clock."

I was at my desk and he was nearby, on one of the straight-backed chairs. Next to him was Maryella, in the wing chair that I like to read in, and on the other side of her was Larry. Then Daniel Huddleston; and ending the arc was Janet in the red leather chair, her shoulders sagging, looking as if she were only about half there. As far as that goes, none of them looked very comfortable, not even Maryella; she would glance at one of them and then look back at Wolfe, and set her teeth on her lip and clear her throat again.

Wolfe's half-open eyes were directed at Brady. "I'm afraid you may be a little late at your office, doctor. I'm sorry—"

"But what kind of a performance is this? You said on the telephone—"

"Please," Wolfe interrupted sharply. "I said that to get you here." His glance went around. "The situation is no longer as I represented it on the phone, to any of you. I told you that it was definitely known that Miss Huddleston had been murdered. Now we're a little further along. I know who murdered her."

They stared at him. Maryella's teeth went deeper into her lip. Janet gripped the arms of her chair and stopped breathing. Daniel leaned forward with his chin stuck out like a halfback waiting for a signal. Brady made a noise in his throat. The only one who uttered anything intelligible was Larry. He said harshly:

"The hell you do."

Wolfe nodded. "I do. That is one change in the situation. The other is that an attempt has been made to murder Miss Nichols.—Please! There is no cause for alarm. The attempt was frustrated—"

"When?" Brady demanded. "What kind of an attempt?"

"To murder Janet!" Maryella exclaimed incredulously.

Wolfe frowned at them. "This will go more quickly and smoothly with no interruptions. I'll make it as brief as possible; I assure you I have no wish to prolong the unpleasantness. Especially since I find less than enjoyable the presence in this room of an extremely unattractive person. I shall call that person X. As you all know, X began with an effort to injure Miss Huddleston by sending anonymous letters—"

"Nothing of the sort!" Larry blurted indignantly. "We don't know that one of us sent those letters! Neither do you!"

"Put it this way, Mr. Huddleston." Wolfe wiggled a finger at him. "I make statements. You suspect belief. In the end there will be a verdict, and you will concur or not. X sent those letters. Then he—I am forced thus to exclude women, at least temporarily, by the pronominal inadequacy of our language—then he became dissatisfied with the results, or something happened, no matter which. In any case, X decided on something more concrete and conclusive. Murder. The technique was unquestionably suggested by the recent death of Miss Horrocks by tetanus. A small amount of material procured at the stable, immersed in water, furnished the required emulsion. It was strained and mixed with argyrol, the mixture was put in a bottle with an iodine label, and the bottle was substituted for the iodine bottle in the cabinet in Miss Huddleston's bathroom. But—"

"Her bathroom?" Maryella was incredulous again.

"Yes, Miss Timms. But X was not one to wait indefinitely for some accidental disjunction in Miss Huddleston's skin. He carried the preparations further, by smashing her bottle of bath salts and inserting a sliver of glass among the bristles of her bath brush. Beautifully simple. It would be supposed that the sliver lodged there when the bottle broke. If she saw it and removed it, no harm done, try again. If she didn't see it, she would cut herself, and there was the iodine bottle—"

"Nuts!" Larry exploded. "You can't possibly—"

"No?" Wolfe snapped. "Archie, if you please?"

I took it from my pocket and handed it to him, and he displayed it to them between his thumb and forefinger. "Here it is. The identical piece of glass."

They craned their necks. Brady stretched clear out of his chair, demanding, "How in the name of God—"

"Sit down, Dr. Brady. How did I get it? We'll come to that. Those were the preparations. But chance intervened, to make better ones. That very afternoon, on the terrace, a tray of glasses was upset and the pieces flew everywhere. X conceived a brilliant improvisation on the spot. Helping to collect the pieces, he deposited one in Miss Huddleston's slipper, and, entering the house on an errand, as all of you did in connection with that minor catastrophe, he ran upstairs and removed the sliver of glass from the bath brush, and got the bogus bottle of iodine, took it downstairs, and placed it in the cupboard in the living room, removing the genuine one kept there. For an active person half a minute, at most a minute, did for that."

Wolfe sighed. "As you know, it worked. Miss Huddleston stuck her foot in the slipper and cut her toe, her brother brought the iodine, Dr. Brady applied it, and she got tetanus and died." His eyes darted to Brady. "By the way, doctor, that suggests a question. Is it worthy of remark that you failed to notice the absence of the characteristic odor of iodine? I merely ask."

Brady was looking grim. "As far as I am concerned," he said acidly, "it remains to be proven that the bottle did not contain iodine, and therefore—"

"Nonsense. I told you on the phone. The piece of turf where the chimpanzee poured some of the contents has been analyzed. Argyrol, no iodine, and a surfeit of tetanus germs. The police have it. I tell you, I tell all of you, that however disagreeable you may find this inquiry as I pursue it, it would be vastly more disagreeable if the police were doing it. Your alternative—"

The doorbell called me away, since Fritz had been told to leave it to me. I dashed out, not wanting to miss anything crucial, and naturally took the precaution, under the circumstances, of pulling the curtain aside for a peek through the glass. It was well that I did. I never saw the stoop more officially populated. Inspector Cramer, Lieutenant Rowcliff, and Sergeant Stebbins! I slipped the chain bolt in place, which would let the door come only five inches, turned the lock and the knob and pulled, and spoke through the crack:

"They don't live here any more."

"Listen, you goddamn squirt," Cramer said impolitely. "Open the door!"

"Can't. The hinge is broke."

"I say open up! We know they're here!"

"You do in a pig's eye. The things you *don't* know. If you've got one, show it. No? No warrant? And all the judges out to lunch—"

"By God, if you think—"

"I don't. Mr. Wolfe thinks. All I have is brute force. Like this—"

I banged the door to, made sure the lock had caught, went to the kitchen and stood on a chair and removed a screw, bolted the back door and told Fritz to leave it that way, and returned to the office. Wolfe stopped talking to look at me. I nodded, and told him as I crossed to my chair:

"Three irate men. They'll probably return with legalities."

"Who are they?"

"Cramer, Rowcliff, Stebbins."

"Ha." Wolfe looked gratified. "Disconnect the bell."

"Done."

"Bolt the back door."

"Done."

"Good." He addressed them: "An inspector, a lieutenant, and a sergeant of police have this building under siege. Since they are investigating murder, and since all of the persons involved have been collected here by me and they know it, my bolted doors will irritate them almost beyond endurance. I shall let them enter when I am ready, not before. If any of you wish to leave now, Mr. Goodwin will let you out to the street. Do you?"

Nobody moved or spoke, or breathed.

Wolfe nodded. "During your absence, Archie, Dr. Brady stated that outdoors on that terrace, with a breeze going, it is not likely that the absence of the iodine odor would have been noticed by him, or by anyone. Is that correct, doctor?"

"Yes," Brady said curtly.

"Very well. I agree with you." Wolfe surveyed the group. "So X's improvisation was a success. Later, of course, he replaced the genuine iodine in the cupboard and removed the bogus. From his standpoint, it was next to perfect. It might indeed have been perfect, invulnerable to any inquest, if the chimpanzee hadn't poured some of that mixture on the grass. I don't know why X didn't attend to that; there was plenty of time, whole days and nights; possible he hadn't seen the chimpanzee doing it, or maybe he didn't realize the danger. And we know he was foolhardy. He should certainly have disposed of the bogus iodine and the piece of glass he had removed from Miss Huddleston's bath brush when it was no longer needed, but he didn't. He—"

"How do you know he didn't?" Larry demanded.

"Because he kept them. He must have kept them, since he used them. Yesterday he put the bogus iodine in the cabinet in Miss Nichols' bathroom, and the piece of glass in her bath brush."

I was watching them all at once, or trying to, but he or she was too good for me. The one who wasn't surprised and startled put on so good an imitation of it that I was no better off than I was before. Wolfe was taking them in too, his narrowed eyes the only moving part of him, his arms folded, his chin on his necktie.

"And," he rumbled, "it worked. This morning. Miss Nichols got in the tub, cut her arm, took the bottle from the cabinet, and applied the stuff—"

"Good God!" Brady was out of his chair. "Then she must—"

Wolfe pushed a palm at him. "Calm yourself, doctor. Antitoxin has been administered."

"By whom?"

"By a qualified person. Please be seated. Thank you. Miss Nichols does not need your professional services, but

I would like to use your professional knowledge. First—Archie, have you got that brush?"

It was on my desk, still wrapped in the paper Hoskins had got for me. I removed the paper and offered the brush to Wolfe, but instead of taking it he asked me:

"You use a bath brush, don't you? Show us how you manipulate it. On your arm."

Accustomed as I was to loony orders from him, I merely obeyed. I started at the wrist and made vigorous sweeps to the shoulder and back.

"That will do, thank you.—No doubt all of you, if you use bath brushes, wield them in a similar manner. Not, that is, with a circular motion, or around the arm, but lengthwise, up and down. So the cut on Miss Nichols's arm, as Mr. Goodwin described it to me, runs lengthwise, about halfway between the wrist and the elbow. Is that correct, Miss Nichols?"

Janet nodded, cleared her throat, and said, "Yes," in a small voice.

"And it's about an inch long. A little less?"

"Yes."

Wolfe turned to Brady. "Now for you, sir. Your professional knowledge. To establish a premise invulnerable to assault. Why did Miss Nichols carve a gash nearly an inch long on her arm? Why didn't she jerk the brush away the moment she felt her skin being ruptured?"

"Why?" Brady was scowling at him. "For the obvious reason that she didn't feel it."

"Didn't feel it?"

"Certainly not. I don't know what premise you're trying to establish, but with the bristles rubbing her skin there would be no feeling of the sharp glass cutting her. None whatever. She wouldn't know she had been cut until she saw the blood."

"Indeed." Wolfe looked disappointed. "You're sure of that? You'd testify to it?"

"I would. Positively."

"And any other doctor would?"

"Certainly."

"Then we'll have to take it that way. Those, then, are the facts. I have finished. Now it's your turn to talk. All of you. Of course this is highly unorthodox, all of you together like this, but it would take too long to do it properly, singly."

He leaned back and joined his finger tips at the apex of his central magnificence. "Miss Timms, we'll start with you. Talk, please."

Maryella said nothing. She seemed to be meeting his gaze, but she didn't speak.

"Well, Miss Timms?"

"I don't know—" she tried to clear the huskiness from her voice—"I don't know what you want me to say."

"Nonsense," Wolf said sharply. "You know quite well. You are an intelligent woman. You've been living in that house two years. It is likely that ill feeling or fear, any emotion whatever, was born in one of these people and distended to the enormity of homicide, and you were totally unaware of it? I don't believe it. I want you to tell me the things that I would drag out of you if I kept you here all afternoon firing questions at you."

Maryella shook her head. "You couldn't drag anything out of me that's not in me."

"You won't talk?"

"I can't talk." Maryella did not look happy. "When I've got nothing to say."

Wolfe's eyes left her. "Miss Nichols?"

Janet shook her head.

"I won't repeat it. I'm saying to you what I said to Miss Timms."

"I know you are." Janet swallowed and went on in a thin voice, "I can't tell you anything, honestly I can't."

"Not even who tried to kill you? You have no idea who tried to kill you this morning?"

"No—I haven't. That's what frightened me so much. I don't know who it was."

Wolfe grunted, and turned to Larry. "Mr. Huddleston?"

"I don't know a damn thing," Larry said gruffly.

"You don't. Dr. Brady?"

"It seems to me," Brady said coolly, "that you stopped before you were through. You said you know who murdered Miss Huddleston. If—"

"I prefer to do it this way, doctor. Have you anything to tell me?"

"No."

"Nothing with any bearing on any aspect of this business?"

"No."

Wolfe's eyes went to Daniel "Mr. Huddleston, you have already talked, to me and to the police. Have you anything new to say?"

"I don't think I have," Daniel said slowly. He looked more miserable than anyone else. "I agree with Dr. Brady that if you—"

"I would expect you to," Wolfe snapped. His glance swept the arc. "I warn all you, with of course one exception, that the police will worm it out of you and it will be a distressing experience. They will make no distinction between relevancies and irrelevancies. They will, for example, impute significance to the fact that Miss Timms has been trying to captivate Mr. Larry Huddleston with her charms—"

"I have not!" Maryella cried indignantly. "Whatever—"

"Yes, you have. At least you did on Tuesday, August

19th. Mr. Goodwin is a good reporter. Sitting on the arm of his chair. Ogling him—"

"I wasn't! I wasn't trying to captivate him—"

"Do you love him? Desire him? Fancy him?"

"I certainly don't!"

"Then the police will be doubly suspicious. They will suspect that you were after him for his aunt's money. And speaking of money, some of you must know that Miss Huddleston's brother was getting money from her and dissatisfied with what he got. Yet you refuse to tell me—"

"I wasn't dissatisfied," Daniel broke in. His face flushed and his voice rose. "You have no right to make insinuations—"

"I'm not making insinuations." Wolfe was crisp. "I am showing you the sort of thing the police will get their teeth into. They are quite capable of supposing you were blackmailing your sister—"

"Blackmail!" Daniel squealed indignantly. "She gave it to me for research—"

"Research!" his nephew blurted with a sneer. "Research! The Elixir of Life! Step right up, gents . . ."

Daniel sprang to his feet, and for a second I thought his intention was to commit mayhem on Larry, but it seemed he merely was arising to make a speech.

"That," he said, his jaw quivering with anger, "is a downright lie! My motivation and my methods are both strictly scientific. Elixir of Life is a romantic and inadmissible conception. The proper scientific term is 'catholicon.' My sister agreed with me, and being a woman of imagination and insight, for years she generously financed—"

"Catholicon!" Wolfe was staring at him incredulously. "And I said you were capable of using your brains!"

"I assure you, sir—"

"Don't try. Sit down." Wolfe was disgusted. "I don't care if you wasted your sister's money, but there are some things you people know that I do care about, and you are foolish not to tell me." He wiggled a finger at Brady. "You, doctor, should be ashamed of yourself. You ought to know better. It is idiotic to withhold facts which are bound to be uncovered sooner or later. You said you had nothing to tell me with any bearing on any aspect of this business. What about the box of stable refuse you procured for the stated purpose of extracting tetanus germs from it?"

Daniel made a noise and turned his head to fix Brady with a stare. Brady was taken aback, but not as much as might have been expected. He regarded Wolfe a moment and then said quietly, "I admit I should have told you that."

"Is that all you have to say about it? Why didn't you tell the police when they first started to investigate?"

"Because I thought there was nothing to investigate. I continued to think so until this morning, when you phoned me. It would have served no useful purpose—"

"What did you do with that stuff?"

"I took it to the office and did some experiments with two of my colleagues. We were settling an argument. Then we destroyed it. All of it."

"Did any of these people know about it?"

"I don't—" Brady frowned. "Yes, I remember—I discussed it. Telling them how dangerous any small cut might be—"

"Not me," Daniel said grimly. "If I had known you did that—"

They glared at each other. Daniel muttered something and sat down.

The phone rang, and I swiveled and got it. It was Doc Vollmer, and I nodded to Wolfe and he took it. When he hung up he told them:

"The bottle from which Miss Nichols treated her wound this morning contained enough tetanus germs to destroy the population of a city, properly distributed." He focused on Brady. "You may have some idea, doctor, how the police would regard that episode, especially if you had withheld it. It would give you no end of trouble. In a thing like this evasion or concealment should never be attempted without the guidance of an expert. By the way, how long had you known Miss Huddleston?"

"I had known her casually for some time. Several years."

"How long intimately?"

"I wouldn't say I knew her intimately. A couple of months ago I formed the habit of going there rather often."

"What made you form the habit? Did you fall in love with her?"

"With whom?"

"Miss Huddleston."

"Certainly not." Brady looked not only astonished but insulted. "She was old enough to be my mother."

"Then why did you suddenly start going there?"

"Why—a man goes places, that's all."

Wolfe shook his head. "Not in an emotional vacuum. Was it greed or parsimony? Free horseback rides? I doubt it; your income is probably adequate. Mere convenience? No; it was out of your way, quite a bother. My guess, to employ the conventional euphemism, is love. Had you fallen in love with Miss Nichols?"

"No."

"Then what? I assure you, doctor, I am doing this much more tactfully than the police would. What was it?"

A funny look appeared on Brady's face. Or a series of looks. First it was denial, then hesitation, then embarrassment, then do or die. All the time his eyes were straight at Wolfe. Suddenly he said, in a voice louder than he had been using, "I had fallen in love with Miss Timms. Violently."

"Oh!" Maryella exclaimed in amazement. "You certainly never—"

"Don't interrupt, please," Wolfe said testily. "Had you notified Miss Timms of your condition?"

"No, I hadn't." Brady stuck to his guns. "I was afraid to. She was so—I didn't suppose—she's a terrible flirt—"

"That's not true! You know mighty well—"

"Please!" Wolfe was peremptory. His glance shot from right to left and back again. "So all but one of you knew of Dr. Brady's procuring that box of material from the stable, and all withheld the information from me. You're hopeless. Let's try another one, more specific. The day Miss Huddleston came here, she told me that Miss Nichols had a grievance against her, and she suspected her of sending those anonymous letters. I ask all of you—including you, Miss Nichols—what was that grievance?"

No one said a word.

"I ask you individually. Miss Nichols?"

Janet shook her head. Her voice was barely audible. "Nothing. It was nothing."

"Mr. Huddleston?"

Daniel said promptly, "I have no idea."

"Miss Timms?"

"I don't know," Maryella said, and by the way Wolfe's eyes stayed with her an instant, I saw that he knew she was lying.

"Dr. Brady?"

"If I knew I'd tell you," Brady said, "but I don't."

"Mr. Huddleston?"

Larry was waiting for him with a fixed smile that twisted a corner of his mouth. "I told you before," he said harshly, "that I don't know a damn thing. That goes right down the line."

"Indeed. May I have your watch a moment, please?"

Larry goggled at him.

"That hexagonal thing on your wrist," Wolfe said. "May I see it a moment?"

Larry's face displayed changes, as Brady's had shortly before. First it was puzzled, then defiant, then he seemed to be pleased about something. He snarled:

"What do you want with my watch?"

"I want to look at it. It's a small favor. You haven't been very helpful so far."

Larry, his lips twisted with the smile again, unbuckled the strap and arose to pass the watch across the desk to Wolfe, whose fingers closed over it as he said to me:

"The Huddleston folder, Archie."

I went and unlocked the cabinet and got out the folder and brought it. Wolfe took it and flipped it open and said:

"Stay there, Archie. As a bulwark and a witness. Two witnesses would be better. Dr. Brady, if you will please stand beside Mr. Goodwin and keep your eyes on me? Thank you."

Wolfe's eyes went through the gap between Brady and me to focus on Larry. "You are a very silly young man, Mr. Huddleston. Incredibly callow. You were smugly gratified because you thought I was expecting to find a picture of Miss Nichols in your watch case and would be chagrined not to. You were wrong. Now, doctor, and Archie, please observe. Here is the back of the watch. Here is a picture of Miss Nichols, trimmed to six sides, and apparently to fit. The point could be definitely determined by opening the watch case, but I'm not going to, because it will be opened later and microscopically compared with the picture to prove that it did contain it—Archie!"

I bulwarked. I owed Larry a smack anyhow, for bad manners if nothing else, but I didn't actually deliver it, since all he did was shoot off his mouth and try to shove through Brady and me to make a grab for the watch. So I merely stiff-armed him and propelled him backwards into his chair and stood ready.

"So," Wolfe went on imperturbably, "I put the watch and picture inside separate envelopes for safekeeping. Thus. If, Mr. Huddleston, you are wondering how I got that picture, your aunt left it here. I suggest that it is time for you to help us a little, and I'll start with a question that I can make a test of. When did your aunt take that picture from you?"

Larry was trying to sneer, but it wasn't working very well. His face couldn't hold it because some of the muscles were making movements of their own.

"Probably," Wolfe said, "it's time to let the police in. I suppose they'll get along faster with you—"

"You fat bastard!" But the snarl in Larry's voice had become a whine.

Wolfe grimaced. "I'll try once more, sir. You are going to answer these questions, if not for me then for someone less fat but more importunate. Would you rather have it dug out of the servants and your friends and acquaintances? It's shabby enough as it is; that would only make it worse. When did your aunt take that picture from you?"

Larry's jaw worked, but his tongue didn't. Wolfe waited ten seconds, then said curtly:

"Let them in, Archie."

I took a step, but before I took another one Larry blurted:

"Goddamn you! You know damn well when she took it! She took it the day she came down here!"

Wolfe nodded. "That's better. But that wasn't the first time she objected to your relations with Miss Nichols. Was it?"

"No."

"Did she object on moral grounds?"

"Hell, no. She objected to our getting married. She

ordered me to break off the engagement. The engagement was secret, but she got suspicious and questioned Janet, and Janet told her, and she made me call it off."

"And naturally you were engaged." Wolfe's voice was smooth, silky. "You burned for revenge—"

"I did not!" Larry leaned forward, having trouble to control his jaw. "You can come off that right now! You're not going to pin anything on me! I never really wanted to marry her, and what's more, I never intended to! I can prove that by a friend of mine!"

"Indeed." Wolfe's eyes were nearly shut. "A man like you has friends? I suppose so. But after your aunt made you break the engagement you still kept the picture in your watch?"

"Yes. I had to. I mean I had Janet to deal with too, and it wasn't easy, living right there in the house. I was afraid of her. You don't know her. I opened the watch case purposely in front of my aunt so she'd take that damn picture. Janet seemed to think the picture meant something, and I thought when she knew it was gone—"

"Did you know that Miss Nichols sent the anonymous letters?"

"No, I didn't. Maybe I suspected, but I didn't know."

"Did you also suspect, when your aunt—"

"Stop! Stop it!"

It was Janet.

She didn't raise her voice. She didn't have to. The tone alone was enough to stop anything and anybody. It was what you would expect to come out of an old abandoned grave, if you had such expectations. Except her mouth, no part of her moved. Her eyes were concentrated on Wolfe's face, with an expression in them that made it necessary for me to look somewhere else. Apparently it had the same effect on the others, for they did the same as me. We gazed at Wolfe.

"Ha," he said quietly. "A little too much for you, is it, Miss Nichols?"

She went on staring at him.

"As I expected," he said, "you're all rubble inside. There's nothing left of you. The simplest way is for me to dictate a confession and you sign it. Then I'll send a copy of it to a man I know, the editor of the *Gazette*, and it will be on his front page this evening. He would like an exclusive picture of you to go with it, and Mr. Goodwin will be glad to take it. I know you'll like that."

Uh-huh, I thought, he's not only going to make a monkey of Cramer, he's going to give him a real black eye. Daniel muttered something, and so did Brady, but Wolfe silenced them with a gesture.

"For your satisfaction," he went on, "I ought to tell you, Miss Nichols, that your guilt was by no means obvious. I became aware of it only when Mr. Goodwin telephoned me from Riverdale this morning, though I did of course notice Mr. Larry Huddleston's hexagonal watch when he came here nine days ago, and I surmised your picture had been in it. But your performance today was the act of a nitwit. I presume you were struck with consternation yesterday when you saw that turf being removed, realized what the consequences would be, and attempted to divert suspicion by staging an attack on yourself. Did you know what I was getting at a while ago when I asked Dr. Brady why you didn't jerk the brush away the instant you felt the glass puncture your skin? And he replied, as of course he would, that you didn't feel the glass cutting you?"

She didn't answer.

"That," Wolfe said, "was precisely the point, that you did jerk the brush away when you had pulled it along your arm less than an inch, because you knew the glass was there and was cutting you, having put it there yourself.

Otherwise the cut would have been much longer, probably half the length of your arm. You saw Mr. Goodwin wield the brush as an illustration, sweeping from wrist to shoulder. Everyone does that. At least, no one moves the brush less than an inch and stops. But even without that, your performance today was fantastic, if you meant—as you did—to make it appear as an attempt by some other person to kill you. Such a person would have known that after what had happened, even if you used the bogus iodine, you would certainly have antitoxin administered, which would have made the attempt a fiasco. Whereas you, arranging the affair yourself, knew that a dose of antitoxin would save you from harm. You really—"

"Stop it!" Janet said, in exactly the same tone as before. I couldn't look at her.

But that was a mistake, not looking at her. For completely without warning she turned into a streak of lightning. It was so sudden and swift that I was still in my chair when she grabbed the sliver of glass from Wolfe's desk, and by the time I got going she had whirled and gone through the air straight at Larry Huddleston, straight at his face with the piece of glass in her fingers. Everyone else moved too, but no one fast enough, not even Larry. Daniel got his arms around her, her left arm pinned against her, and I got her other arm, including the wrist, but there was a red streak across Larry's cheek from beneath his eye nearly to his chin.

Everybody but Janet was making noises, some of which were words.

"Shut up!" Wolfe said gruffly. "Archie, if you've finished your nap—"

"Go to hell," I told him. "I'm not a genius like you." I gave Janet's wrist a little pressure. "Drop it, girlie."

She let the piece of glass fall to the floor and stood rigid, watching. Brady examined Larry's cheek.

"Only skin deep," Brady said, unfolding a handkerchief. "Here, hold this against it."

"By God," Larry blurted, "if it leaves a scar—"

"That was a lie," Janet said. "You lied!"

"What?" Larry glared at her.

"She means," Wolfe put in, "that you lied when you said you neither desired nor intended to marry her. I agree with her that the air was already bad enough in here without that. You fed her passion and her hope. She wanted you, God knows why. When your aunt intervened, she struck. For revenge? Yes. Or saying to your aunt, preparing to say, 'Let me have him or I'll ruin you?' Probably. Or to ruin your aunt and then collect you from the debris? Possibly. Or all three, Miss Nichols?"

Janet, her back to him, still facing Larry, did not speak. I held onto her.

"But," Wolfe said, "your aunt came to see me, and that frightened her. Also, when she herself came that evening and found that picture here, the picture you had carried in your watch, she was not only frightened but enraged. Being a very sentimental young woman—"

"Good God," Brady muttered involuntarily. "Sentimental!"

A shudder ran over Janet from top to bottom. I pulled her around by the arm and steered her to the red leather chair and she dropped into it. Wolfe said brusquely:

"Archie, your notebook. No—first the camera—"

"I can't stand it!" Maryella cried, standing up. She reached for something to hold onto, and as luck would have it, it was Brady's arm. "I can't!"

Wolfe frowned at them. "Take her up and show her the orchids, doctor. Three flights. And take that casualty along and patch it up. Fritz will get what you need. I advise you to smell the iodine."

At six o'clock that evening I was at my desk. The office was quiet and peaceful. Wolfe had done it up brown. Cramer had come like a lion with a squad and a warrant, and had departed like a lamb with a flock of statements, a confession, a murderer, and apoplexy. Despite all of which, loving Cramer as I do, when I heard the elevator bringing Wolfe down from the plant rooms I got too busy with my desk work to turn around. Intending not even to acknowledge his presence. The excuse he had given for keeping Maryella there was that it was impossible for her to return to Riverdale as things stood, and there was no place else for her to go. Phooey.

But I got no chance to freeze them out, for they went right on by the office door, to the kitchen. I stuck to my desk. Time went by, but I was too irritated to get any work done. Towards seven o'clock the bell rang, and I went to the front door and found Doc Brady. He said he had been invited, so I took him to the kitchen.

The kitchen was warm, bright, and full of appetizing smells. Fritz was slicing a ripe pineapple. Wolfe was seated in the chair by the window, tasting out of a steaming saucepan. Maryella was perched on one end of the long table with her legs crossed, sipping a mint julep. She fluttered the fingers of her free hand at Brady for a greeting. He stopped in astonishment, and stood and blinked at her, at Wolfe and Fritz, and back at her.

"Well," he said. "Really. I'm glad you can be so festive. Under the circumstances—"

"Nonsense!" Wolfe snapped. "There's nothing festive about it; we're merely preparing a meal. Miss Timms is much better occupied. Would you prefer hysterics? We had a discussion about spoon bread, and there are two batches in the oven. Two eggs, and three eggs. Milk at a hundred and fifty degrees, and boiling. Take that julep she's offering you. Archie, a julep?"

Brady took the julep from her, set it down on the table without sampling it, wrapped his arms around her, and made it tighter. She showed no inclination to struggle or scratch. Wolfe pretended not to notice, and placidly took another taste from the saucepan. Fritz started trimming the slices of pineapple.

Maryella gasped, "Ah think, Ah'd bettah breathe."

Wolfe asked amiably, "A julep, Archie?"

I turned without answering, went to the hall and got my hat, slammed the door from the outside, walked to the corner and into Sam's place, and climbed onto a stool at the counter. I didn't know I was muttering to myself, but I must have been, for Sam, behind the counter, demanded:

"Spoon bread? What the hell is spoon bread?"

"Don't speak till you're spoken to," I told him, "and give me a ham sandwich and a glass of toxin. If you have no toxin, make it milk. Good old wholesome orangutan milk. I have been playing tag with an undressed murderess. Do you know how to tell a murderess when you see one? It's a cinch. Soak her in iodine over night, drain through cheesecloth, add a pound of pig chitlins—what? Oh. Rye and no pickle. Ah think Ah'd bettah breathe."

I have never mentioned it to him, and I don't intend to. I've got a dozen theories about it. Here are a few for samples:

1. He knew I would go to the funeral, and he sent that bunch of orchids purely and simply to pester me.

2. Something from his past. When he was young and handsome, and Bess Huddleston was ditto, they might have been—uh, acquainted. As for her not recognizing him, I doubt if his own mother would, as is. And there's no doubt he has fifteen or twenty pasts; I know that much about him.

3. He was paying a debt. He knew, or had an idea, that she was going to be murdered, from something someone said that first day, and was too damn lazy, or too interested in corned beef hash with chitlins, to do anything about it. Then when she was ready for burial he felt he owed her something, so he sent her what? Just some orchids, any old orchids? No, sir. Black ones. The first black orchids ever seen on a coffin anywhere on the globe since the dawn of history. Debt canceled. Paid in full. File receipted bills.

4. I'll settle for number three.

5. But it's still a mystery, and when he catches me looking at him a certain way he knows darned well what's on my mind.

A. G.